THE DEADLY SITKA SHORE

As he started down the rocky trail, Darby knew he was taking a desperate risk. Bryant must be stopped—permanently—but the unarmed Derby Man had only his strength and stamina to challenge Bryant's loaded gun and evil killer's instincts.

Suddenly Bryant whirled, his gun coming to rest on Darby. "You're not fooling anyone, Buckingham! For you, this is the end."

He cocked his pistol. Darby crouched in the moonlight, staring at the dark silhouette, and the gun that pointed at him, ready to blow away his life.

And, in that last awful moment as he knelt on the stony rubble, he realized that, once again, he'd run out of time and luck.

North Chase

Gary McCarthy

BANTAM BOOKS
TORONTO · NEW YORK · LONDON · SYDNEY

NORTH CHASE
A Bantam Book/February 1982

ISBN 0-553-20116-6

Published simultaneously in the United States and Canada

Bantam Books are published by Bantam Books, Inc. Its trade-
mark, consisting of the words "Bantam Books" and the por-
trayal of a rooster, is Registered in U.S. Patent and Trademark
Office and in other countries. Marca Registrada. Bantam
Books, Inc., 666 Fifth Avenue, New York, New York 10103.

For Richard R. Smith,
who has been there.

North Chase

Chapter 1

Darby Buckingham was on the first Central Pacific train into Reno, Nevada. Back at Donner Pass, the workers were still clearing away the debris left by the recent sabotage explosion. But that was behind him. He'd helped the railroad's backers whip the mighty Sierras and now he was enjoying his just rewards.

The eastern dime novelist was in his very best attire as he lounged in the sumptuous coach provided by Charles Crocker himself. His black coat and pants had been freshly cleaned and pressed by the Chinese whom he'd befriended in the earliest stages of the railroad's construction. Darby's gold pocket watch and chain were evidence of his considerable income, and his glistening black shoes reflected that prosperity; atop his head the famous derby was aligned at its usual jaunty angle.

Everything was ready for the celebration. Even now, the sound of the Reno Municipal Band reached his ears as it struck up a splashy rendition of "She'll Be Comin' Around The Mountain."

The writer grinned at himself in the mirror. His moustache, black as tar and thick as a barn-brush, was trimmed and waxed at the tips. His eyes showed fatigue, but that would vanish during the long awaited vacation he and Dolly Beavers would soon be enjoying together in San Francisco. His trousers *did* sag, however, and that caused a hint of annoyance to etch into his strong features.

He'd lost over twenty pounds working on the Central Pacific. At 5'9" and now weighing only 235 pounds, he thought of himself as gaunt and half-starved in appearance.

1

Ah, but the San Francisco cuisine was famous and he'd soon put it back on, because never in the entire history of the Buckinghams had one ever allowed himself to appear less than robust. It was simply inconceivable that a man of reputation for both strength and ferocity could slip to ordinary proportions.

He felt the train begin to slow down. It was a warm spring day and, after the blizzards he'd faced on Donner Summit, it seemed almost as if he were entering a tropical paradise.

The train eased by crowds of waving Nevadans. These were jubilant people who realized that the new railroad would make Reno prosperous and bring them goods from California at unheard of prices. No longer would supplies from the east coast be freighted over the mountains by wagon. No longer, too, would these townspeople be locked away from the refinements of San Francisco because of the rigors of stagecoach travel and the capricious winter storms. Their world had instantly expanded a hundredfold with the coming of the railroad.

Darby actually beamed through the window at them. He lit one of his rich Cuban cigars and toasted their applause with a crystal snifter of brandy. Nearby, a tub full of Sierra ice held three bottles of champagne for the private celebration he'd soon have with Miss Dolly Beavers.

The writer imprinted the details of this historic arrival in his mind; later, he would record it for posterity in his upcoming novel. What a triumph this was! Remember how Congress and half the nation had said they'd never even get over the mountains? To the east stretched the great reaches of Nevada, waiting to be spanned as the railroad crews hurried to join the approaching Union Pacific Railroad. Yes, the great race was on!

He grinned. Wait until he told Dolly that Charles Crocker himself had awarded him the honor of telegraphing the message of their victory directly to President Andrew Johnson!

The train shuddered to a halt with every car on the line creaking and groaning like a thousand frozen hinges bending. Big hissing clouds of steam momentarily obliterated and incapacitated the Reno Municipal Band as instruments clashed against one another in brassy confusion.

When the steam finally evaporated, Darby saw a raised platform of choking dignitaries. He grinned impishly at the scene of chaos, then he spotted Dolly in their midst and his cigar dropped absently into his lap. What a woman! What a dress! It was purple, with a neckline that was enough to make his palms sweat. She had the figure of the Greek Goddess of Love and there were little ribbons entwined in her flowing blonde hair; her face was perfect enough to make angels weep with envy. He gaped with admiration as Dolly Beavers jumped up and down on the stand for several moments until he realized every other man on the platform was enjoying her sprightly performance, too. Lascivious worms!

Darby flew out of his seat and charged the exit, unmindful of the hole his cigar had burned in his suit.

When the crowd saw the handsome pair unite in a violent embrace, they unleashed a great cheer. Darby scarcely heard the band as it lurched into another tune. He normally wasn't a man to demonstrate his affections in public, but it sure felt good to hold this woman.

"Oh, Derby!" she panted when finally their lips suctioned apart. "Never leave me again!"

He gazed deep into her blue eyes. "I never really did," he said. "Not in my. . . ."

Dolly's reaction was one of instant amazement. She blinked, pushed back a little and demanded, "Then what do you call eight months up on a mountain?"

"I meant in my *heart*, dear."

She had a comeback but, fortunately, the Mayor of Reno jammed a gold-painted wooden key between them saying, "Umph, I . . . I hate to intrude on such a touching moment, but if you would allow me to say a few welcoming words for the public and press?"

Darby sighed with relief. *Now* he was beginning to remember how he'd summoned the courage to leave this voluptuous beauty for a time. "Of course, Mayor."

The politician was a gaunt, balding man with mutton-chops and rather sharp, tobacco-stained teeth; he showed them right back to his molars when he grinned down at the expectant faces of Reno voters.

"Ladies and gentlemen!" he bellowed, biting off each word as though his secret desire was to become a Shakespearean actor. "It is my official honor to give this here golden key to our city to the man whose exploits all of you who can read have no doubt seen in the newspaper—Mister Darby Buckingham!"

There was rousing applause and Darby took the key, absently noting how badly one side of it was flyspecked. He raised the clean side up with one hand. "Thank you!" he yelled, pumping the Mayor's fingers with the other. "It is indeed a great honor for me to accept the golden key to your city. As you know from my on-the-scene accounts published in your newspaper, we fought a difficult fight. There were no fewer than sixteen blizzards which. . . ."

"Could you *please* slow down, Mister Buckingham?" pleaded a tall, young red-haired reporter who struggled mightily to hold his note pad and write at the same time.

Darby scowled, but he did attempt to speak more slowly. Even so, the young man didn't seem to be having much success. He was, Darby noted, quite hungry-looking, although his color was good. What was especially intriguing was his clothing—it was similar to Darby's except that it was a peculiar shade of green. His eyebrows were finely etched for such a strong jaw line and his moustache was as red as his hair, though much thinner than Darby's, like the man himself. Darby recognized the fist-busted nose of a man who'd failed to duck—strangely, it enhanced the reporter's appearance with a touch of ruggedness. He suspected the man to be Irish, and he probably couldn't fight any better than he could take notes.

Darby cleared his throat, giving the reporter a couple of extra seconds before continuing. "The sixteen blizzards forced our valiant Chinese crews to assault Summit Tunnel both day and night. We had three shifts. . . ."

4

In his haste, the young reporter's note pad jumped from his long bony fingers to land under the platform.

"Mister Buckingham!" he cried, "I beg you once again, wait just a moment!"

Darby's mouth crimped with annoyance as the reporter ducked under the platform to grab his pad. Suddenly, there was a loud THUNK. The entire platform shook and everyone heard the reporter's grunt of pain. The speech instantly forgotten, Darby and everyone on the grandstand stared in amazement as the impertinent young man, green eyes glazed with pain, held his smashed derby and reeled dazedly into view. A trickle of blood high on his forehead left no doubt as to his discomfort.

"Steady the fool!" Darby growled. "And someone retrieve his note pad and pencil before the clumsy buffoon does himself even more damage."

Dolly Beavers leaned close. "The *poor* dear. He is a *handsome* one, though, isn't he?"

Darby muttered something unprintable. Perhaps now he could continue the account without interruptions. "Our greatest obstacle, besides the Pass, undoubtedly was Cape Horn. And, if it hadn't been for the Chinese allowing themselves to be lowered in reed baskets over the side, high above the American River, we'd. . . ."

"Excuse me!" gasped the reeling reporter once more as he grimly fumbled to hold his pencil.

Darby's eyes sparked and his moustache twitched its dangerous warning. "What," he growled ominously, "is your name?"

"Connor, sir! Connor B. O'Grady."

"What do you want this time, Mister O'Grady? If I'm still talking too fast, I suggest you copy one of these other gentlemen's notes."

There was nervous laughter and O'Grady's face went chalky with humiliation. "I beg your pardon, sir, but you and I know the *real* story of the Sierra crossing was the sabotage attempt by one of Charles Crocker's very own lieutenants. Is it not true that Mister Crocker was betrayed

5

by one of those he most deeply trusted? And wasn't his name Wesley Bryant?''

The other reporters stopped writing. Note pads suddenly forgotten, they leaned forward with anticipation. Darby glared at O'Grady with unconcealed rage. But the question hung over them all in ominous silence. This, he believed, was not the time nor the occasion to make the sabotage public. Today was meant to be a celebration, not an inquisition.

"Perhaps," Darby whispered, "you have failed to understand that the *real* story concerns the brave men who fought and even died to bring our train to this very point, where now we are about to begin the greatest race ever staged in this country!"

The redhead's green eyes flashed with anger. "Why don't you tell everyone the truth," he demanded, "which is that the saboteur himself was blown to pieces at Summit Tunnel by you! That's what we all want to hear about . . ." he paused with a great sense of timing, ". . . or are you saving that story for your *own* western readership?"

Darby's fists knotted. Enough was enough! He pivoted, searching for the stairs which would lead him down to this insolent young fool.

But before he could tear himself free of Dolly, the Mayor cried, "Sheriff Eakins, arrest that man for creating a public disturbance!"

Instantly, the Sheriff and two of his deputies launched themselves off the platform. All three moved in on the tall reporter, who was staring right at Darby with accusing eyes.

When Eakins latched onto the Irishman, the reporter attempted to break free. One of the deputies slugged him along the side of the head. O'Grady roared and walloped the deputy in the stomach as the other one drew his gun.

A woman screamed and her voice made O'Grady spin around and lash the second deputy with a fine straight right to the jaw that had enough kick in it to send the man goosestepping backward.

6

Bravo! Darby thought with grudging admiration as young O'Grady was finally subdued by an aroused crowd who had to pile on him en masse.

"Get him to my jail!" Eakins raged, spittle flying.

"Don't hurt him," Dolly Beavers cried angrily. "Sheriff, don't you dare pistol-whip that young man."

Eakins whirled about in anger.

"She's right," Darby warned. "He doesn't deserve a beating."

The Sheriff wanted to argue, but the warning in Darby's voice stilled his protest, then made him stomp away.

Darby shook his head in wonder. "For a thin chap, he sure put up a good fight. That uppercut he threw wasn't learned in a barroom. He's had some professional tutoring."

The Mayor wasn't impressed. In fact, he looked more than put out. "He's a troublemaker, that one. Stopped by my very own house last night to call on my daughter, Amy. You'd better believe I told him where to go! We don't take to forward-acting strangers in our city."

Darby bottled up the impulse to tell his own thoughts. Instead, he asked, "What newspaper does he work for?"

"Who cares? My own feeling is that he's one of those pushy easterners—probably from New York City."

"*I'm* from New York City," Darby rumbled.

The Mayor's Adam's apple bubbled up and down his turkey-like neck. He grinned and the sharp yellow teeth clicked like Chinese dice. "Ah...ah yes, but you're different. You're the Derby Man."

Darby forgot his next words because, just as he was about to comment, Connor B. O'Grady burst free of his captors.

"Look out!" Eakins squawked. "Don't let the sumbitch get away!"

But O'Grady obviously had no intention of running. He backed up to a wall and motioned them all to come and take him.

"Strike up the band!" the Mayor cried. "Oh, damn him anyway!"

7

In spite of himself, the famous novelist grinned. Young O'Grady had just executed a beautiful overhand right to Eakins' jaw that had laid the Sheriff out cold.

One of the deputies fired into the air and yelled, "Hands up!"

Darby held his breath until he saw the redhead slowly raise his long arms. Beside the writer, Dolly Beavers sighed with relief.

"They'll keep him in that cell until he's an old man," she said with despair.

She looked so upset, Darby said, "I'll go by the Sheriff's office. Maybe . . . maybe, I'll see if he can be freed on bail."

"This is just between us, Mister Buckingham, but as Mayor I can tell you this—the only way we'll consider letting that wild man free is if he leaves Reno for keeps."

Darby nodded. He figured the Mayor's daughter must be pretty good-looking to upset her father so. Not that it mattered. Everyone had their hidden reasons for things. In truth, Darby had to admit that the young redhead had been more than a little correct in his assertion that Wesley Bryant had nearly destroyed the Central Pacific Railroad. But dammit anyway, Darby rationalized, I'm the one who risked my life to get the real story and, therefore, I ought to be the one to tell it. Besides, what good was it in the hands of a young, green-clad Irishman who couldn't even take decent notes?

Darby lit another cigar. Suddenly, he was impatient to get back on the train and be alone with Dolly Beavers. But he knew it would be a while before the switching was completed and the locomotive refueled.

"Can't we get on with whatever you have planned, Mayor?"

"Yes. Yes, of course." The Mayor drew himself up on the balls of his feet and smiled. "And now, ladies and gentlemen, we regret the disturbance but shall get on with our own glorious day in history." With a flourish far more dramatic than the situation called for, the little Mayor unveiled a telegraph apparatus which had been especially wired to the platform.

"We're going to send the message from here?"

"Yes. The city fathers and I have declared today a public holiday so that our children could attend this momentous event."

"Very well." Darby watched a pink-cheeked young lad with a nervous smile bound up the steps to join them, then take his seat crouched over the telegraph key. The spectators leaned forward in rapt attention.

"Now, Mister Buckingham, if you'll just read your Presidential message...."

The sound of splintering wood and glass spun everyone around as, up the street, a man crashed through the front window of the Sheriff's office and young O'Grady catapulted through the door, only to be tackled before he'd staggered to his feet.

"It's him again!" the Mayor shrieked, his face a mask of outrage.

There was a violent scuffle. Shouted voices drifted down the main street. A cry of pain. Then, a rifle's barrel glinted against the sun and arced downward. The struggle was over.

Dolly gripped the dime novelist's arm so hard he winced and pried her fingers loose, then whispered, "Don't worry. I'll see to him before we go."

"Well," the Mayor spat with satisfaction, "that's the end of him! Territorial prison, if I have anything to say about the sentencing. Now, can we finally send your message?"

Darby nodded and reached into his trouser pocket for the wadded note he'd prepared for this occasion. His finger poked through the cigar's burn hole. "Blast!" he hissed.

"Mayor! Something's coming in!" the young telegraph operator cried.

"Well, tell them to shut up 'til we get the Presidential message sent!"

"I . . . I can't!"

"Dammit, boy! Do. . . ."

The operator's hand began to scribble madly on a pad, almost as if he could not stop it from doing an independent work.

"It's important, sir. It's . . . it's from up on Donner Pass."

Darby jumped forward. "Copy it well, son. It may be vital." Then, as they crowded over the rigid young man, this message flowed from the dancing telegraph key:

FROM: Mister Harvey Strobridge, Superintendent of Construction Central Pacific Railroad. STOP.
TO: Mister Darby Buckingham
Special Envoy for U.S. President.
STOP

Do not repeat Do not send Presidential message! STOP. Alarming discovery made less than fifteen minutes ago. STOP. Please return to Donner Pass. STOP. Crocker needs you. Situation critical. Hurry. STOP.

Darby stood transfixed. The telegraph went silent and the operator's hand quivered over the lifeless keys.

"That's all?" Darby whispered.

"Yes, sir."

The writer crushed his own message and hurled it to the floor as Dolly cried, "What does it mean?"

"God only knows," Darby said, feeling dread course through his veins. Harvey Strobridge was not one to panic. Something catastrophic must have happened.

"Boy, wire back Mister Strobridge that we've received his message and that I'll be bringing the train back up just as soon as we take on wood and water."

"Ask him for specifics!" the Mayor urged. "This town has a right to know if something else has gone wrong!"

Darby stared down at the wadded-up message which someone had already trampled flat. Then he glanced up at the Mayor of Reno. "Sure you do. You'll get the news right after the President. Fair enough?"

The Mayor, not being a total fool, gazed into Darby's flat, expressionless eyes and nervously nodded.

Darby stood with his hands wrapped around the cell bars. "Well, O'Grady, they really worked you over."

The young reporter leaned back on his cot, grinning through split lips. "So, you came because you finally put two and two together and realized who I am."

Darby frowned. "What *are* you talking about?"

Connor O'Grady gingerly touched his split lip. "This lower one is the most important when it comes to kissing the girls," he said with a devilish wink. "You bailing me out of here?"

"I'm not sure I can afford to. It seems the Sheriff is ready to hang you and the Mayor is so worked up about his daughter he's willing to help."

O'Grady's face dropped. "I sure didn't come three thousand miles to rot in a jail cell. Besides, I wouldn't take advantage of that sweet Amy. Heck, I hardly had time to do more than shake her hand like a gentleman."

"Are you one?"

"A gentleman? Sure, when I'm with a lady."

Darby wondered if the Mayor's daughter was a lady but decided not to ask. What did seem likely was that Connor O'Grady had a way with women—a certain flair.

"Where did you learn to fight?" Darby asked.

"So," O'Grady said with obvious pleasure, "you noticed."

"I had ample opportunity. I also saw you get beaten with a rifle barrel. Not very intelligent."

"And you were always an intelligent fighter?" O'Grady stood up, his eyes flashing. "That's not what I heard. They tell me you waded into a scrap no matter what the odds. Now, you're accusing me of stupidity for doing the same."

Darby gripped the cell bars. "Who *are* you?" he demanded. "Where did you come from and who told you about me?"

O'Grady stood up straight and tall. He brushed the dirt from his green suit and carefully placed his green derby hat down until it rested atop the goose egg on his forehead.

"I am newly arrived from Boston. I work for no man because no one has yet asked me to, though that may change in the near future. As to my name, it *is* Connor B. O'Grady. Do you know what the B. stands for?"

"Of course not."

"Buckingham. I'm your cousin."

"Impossible!"

"Oh no! My mother was your father's sister. She was disowned by the family over twenty years ago."

Darby throttled the bars as though he might somehow choke the cold truth from them. "Her name. Give me her name!"

"Edith," came the quick reply.

Darby's head came to rest against the bars. "Yes," he said quietly, "Edith. I remember her well. She was . . . headstrong. A rebel, but a dear woman. When I was a child, she always brought me candy. We thought . . . we thought she'd gone away and died."

O'Grady's voice was calm and unaccusing. "In a way," he said softly, "that's the truth. You see, her parents and your father hated the man she chose to marry. There were terrible words and, in the end, she did elope. So, I imagine the Buckinghams never mentioned her name again."

"My father did. Often. He loved her."

"Then he should have searched for her!" O'Grady cried. "Told her that she could come home. Oh, if you only knew how she wanted to—how we both did."

"You should have."

"I know. But in the beginning, she stayed with her husband out of pride. They lived in Philadelphia and he beat her in his stupid, drunken rages. He finally was knifed in a saloon brawl and she prayed her thanks."

O'Grady took a deep breath. "After that, my mother fled to Boston and her life finally began to change for the better. She got a job as a housekeeper for a respectable family on Beacon Hill."

"She could have returned to the fold."

"But she didn't. My mother was desperately afraid she

would be treated with pity. Something she could never endure. In time, she met my father, Clarence O'Grady. He was a coach and stableman, as fine a hand with horses as I've ever seen. I grew up helping him and, in addition to his height and red hair, I think I've inherited his way with animals."

"You're a horseman?"

"Yes, although my experience is on the English saddle rather than the ones they use out here in the west." O'Grady shrugged. "I'm not here to play cowboy, anyway."

"What about your parents?"

"Both dead a year ago."

"I'm sorry."

"Don't be." O'Grady expelled a deep breath. "My father was a good man. A bit of a brawler—like you, Darby. He was tough, but fair with me. He treated my mother like the saint that she was. When she died, he followed within three months and nothing I nor my brothers and sisters could do would have changed that."

"I see." Darby began to pace the corridor before the cell. "So, you've told me you inherited your size and coloring from Mister O'Grady. You apparently inherited no outward appearance of a Buckingham. You and I could not be physically more apart. Did you inherit anything of your mother?"

"*Yes,*" he swore passionately, "a thousand times, yes! Part of it you saw today. My speed of hand. *Your* speed of hand and that which, in addition to your strength, made you a bare knuckles champion. And I also like to think I've inherited the Buckingham talent for literature."

Darby frowned. "That remains to be seen. You handle pencil and paper like a mop and pail. But no matter. Why did you come here to Reno, Nevada?"

"To follow in your illustrious footsteps, of course. I want to chronicle what's going on out here. Only I'd like to do it with short newspaper pieces and with pictures. Lots of pictures."

"Are you an artist?"

"Nope. I can't draw a stick man or even a straight line. I use a camera."

"With more facility than writing materials, I hope."

O'Grady flushed angrily. "Are you going to keep hounding me about such a small failing?"

Darby looked away. "No," he said finally, "I'm not going to 'hound' you at all. I am deeply sorry that we didn't know each other in years past. Maybe I could have taught you how to eat properly, write under the most trying circumstances and even behave like a gentleman. But there's no time now and I must attend to some urgent business. The train awaits."

"But . . . but, so do I!" O'Grady cried. "Darby, I'm family. You can't leave me here to rot or perhaps even be sent to prison just for a bit of fisticuffs! I came west to join you."

"Then you are presumptuous and have made the trip for nothing. I work alone."

"Yeah. I saw how 'alone' you were with that blonde. I think you are just making excuses because you're afraid I'll write a better story than you."

Darby refused to take the bait. Besides, the challenge was too absurd to argue about. "Do yourself a favor. Go home. If you truly want to write, I'll contact my New York editor and he'll at least read your work at my request."

"Don't do me any favors! I'm sure I'll get lots of material in this jail cell."

Darby slammed out of the jail and into the Sheriff's office. "I want him out tomorrow," he said flatly.

"Not a chance in the world," Eakins snarled.

Darby reached into his coat pocket and pulled out his wallet. "What's your monthly salary?"

"Why . . . why, fifty dollars."

Darby slapped money down on the desk and said, "Take a couple of months off and buy him a ticket east on tomorrow's stage."

The man didn't even put up a show of a struggle. He snatched up the bills. "Why, sure!" he grinned, his face swollen and lopsided. "He's as good as gone!"

Darby poked a stubby finger at the man. "You've heard of me."

The smile vanished. "Yes sir, Mister Derby Man. Reckon most every man in this state has heard of what you've done. How you handle trouble."

"Good," Darby said, a slow smile creasing his lips. "Let's just make certain you don't pocket the money and everyone hears how I turned you inside out."

Eakins' face drained white. Darby left him sitting there to think about it and his mind turned to other, more desperate matters.

Something was wrong up in those mountains. Something terrible enough to kill a message for the President. He'd better get on that train and thunder back up to whatever new catastrophe awaited atop Donner Pass.

Chapter 2

The train was ready. Its boiler was filled and the furnace roared as the steam pressure edged up to 110 pounds and operating level. The engineer impatiently blasted the whistle. Boys on horseback sat astride their nervous ponies, ready to make a race of the departure.

"Dammit, I'm coming," Darby bellowed as he stood beside the coach, trying to extract himself from the nearly hysterical Miss Dolly Beavers.

"You *promised* you'd take me with you to San Francisco!" she wailed. "We've had no time alone together at all."

"I know, but what choice do I have? Try to understand. There's trouble up on Donner Pass. I have to go!"

Dolly released him so suddenly he staggered back, almost tripping on the roadbed. "All right," Dolly yelled, "but whatever trouble is brewing up there on that mountain is nothing compared to the trouble you've got with me. Leave and I swear I'll never see you again! I'll return to Running Springs, Wyoming, where you found me."

"Dolly, you wouldn't."

"Watch me!" she cried, stomping her foot down on a railroad tie. "Not only that, but ... but I'll marry Zack Woolsey or Bear Timberly."

Darby's mouth fell open and his face lost all its color. "Surely, you jest!" he stammered incredulously.

"Go and test me, Derby!"

"But ... but they're each old enough to be your father. They never even bathe. I owe them my life but, even so, I can't let you ruin yours!"

"Then take me." Her voice was softer now, less desper-

16

ate and subtly seductive as she edged closer. "I'm not asking you to marry me—yet. But you can't expect to leave me alone all the time."

He tried to argue. "But it could be dangerous."

"Phooey!" she sniffed, as though danger were a thing she routinely faced.

"Would you really marry one of them?" he asked, trying to fathom the depths of her blue eyes.

"Yes," she whispered.

He gave up. "All right, but you're only coming as far as Donner Pass, where we see what I'm facing."

Dolly erupted with a shout of joy and mashed her lips to his as the train whistle screeched again and again.

"Come on!" he roared over the noise. "Let's go! I've got champagne on ice and we might as well enjoy ourselves while we can!"

Dolly laughed then, laughed in the way of a woman who enjoys life to its fullest.

They swung aboard just as the train lurched away. Darby and Dolly stood on the outside platform, linked arm in arm as they watched Reno and the children's ponies fall slowly behind. The locomotive worked hard and they picked up speed, climbing a gentle grade which would soon grow very steep as they crawled into an eastern foothills leading up to the Sierra Nevadas.

"Look!" Dolly yelled, pointing back at the little town beside the Truckee River.

Darby's eyes narrowed. He saw a buggy burst from the group of young riders and their fading ponies. For a hundred yards or more, it swept along beside the tracks then, with incredible daring, the driver reined the matched pair of fast sorrels hard. The light buggy struck the rails a glancing blow, then smashed down between them, one wheel inside, one out, as it rapidly closed the gap. The driver and passenger were waving madly for the train to halt.

"What are the fools trying to do," he swore, "get themselves killed?"

"Why . . ." Dolly's hand flew to her face, "why, it's

17

the Mayor's daughter and . . . and that young firebrand, Connor O'Grady!''

It was true. Who else wore a green suit and derby? ''Blast! They weren't supposed to release him until tomorrow!''

The buggy was jerking wildly over the half-sunken railroad ties, bouncing like a cork in a raging river.

''They'll kill themselves!'' Dolly yelled. Then she began to motion them away.

But O'Grady, his lean body bent forward, right hand gripping the lines, left arm clutched around the pretty but pale young woman at his side, whooped with merriment and waved in return.

The dime novelist grabbed Dolly's slim wrist. ''Stop it. The imbecile thinks you are urging him on!''

Closer and closer they came, until the distended nostrils of the racing sorrels were merely an arm's length from them.

''Go back!'' Darby roared, as he saw O'Grady lean out and study the roadbed along his side of the track.

''They'll never make it,'' Dolly breathed, hand pressed to her lips in rapt fascination. ''If he swings the team over to the side, they'll flip.''

Darby leaned out from the train and peered up the line. It was what he'd feared. A cutback which pinched in on the tracks. O'Grady was finished, he'd have to. . . .

The Irishman yelled something to the girl, who then suddenly braced herself as O'Grady, waiting until the very last moment, swung the buggy hard right and completely off the roadbed.

''He's gone!'' Darby said with a sigh of relief as the train rumbled through the shallow cut in a hillside.

Dolly nodded. ''He's a wild man. I never saw anyone handle a team of horses like that. Where. . . .''

Her words ended with a sharp intake of breath as the buggy reemerged off to one side, nearly abreast of them now. He'd gone around the hill and still managed to gain!

O'Grady whooped gustily, then sawed the foam-flecked horses toward the train. He put the reins into the girl's hands and kissed her pale but excited face. Then, he reached back and grabbed his bags. A moment later, he was leaping from the buggy and grasping the rail of the platform with such nonchalance that one might have supposed he did these things every day.

"Goodbye, Amy!" he yelled as the buggy began to slow. "I'll come back soon. Give your father my best regards!" He glanced over at Darby and winked. "That ought to ruin his disposition."

The girl must have gotten the message because she laughed outright, then brought the sorrels to rest as the train rounded a bend and closed her from sight.

"Plucky, isn't she!" O'Grady said with a chuckle. "Sure doesn't get it from that pompous father of hers. Never had time to meet her mother, you know. . . ."

"Confound it!" Darby roared. "You could have gotten yourselves killed!"

"Not likely. I told you I learned how to handle a team of horses. Catching this train seemed a whole lot safer than flying off Boston's Beacon hill at wintertime."

Dolly smiled. "You did a remarkable job. Will the young lady be expecting you back soon?"

Connor started to say something, but Darby's forearm locked around his neck as he lifted the reporter and flipped him over the rail as easily as he might have a child. Darby Buckingham wasn't an ex-circus strongman and bare knuckles champion for nothing.

"What are you doing!" Dolly cried.

"I'm making sure the young lady sees him quicker than expected, that's what!"

Connor's long legs thrashed as he hung suspended over the now-blurring roadbed.

"You'll kill him, Darby. Please, we're going too fast!"

Darby peered over the railing. They *were* moving at a pretty good rate. He'd never forgive himself if he was the cause of his own cousin's death. No matter how deserving. So with great reluctance, Darby lifted the choking young man back to safety.

"All right," he said angrily, "but when we reach

19

Donner Pass, you are taking the first train back to Reno.''

O'Grady was in no condition to protest. He massaged his neck. ''You stretched it,'' he wheezed in an accusing voice.

''If you don't shape up, someone will do it permanently, with a rope. Now, pass through this coach and go into the next and wait.''

Connor nodded, picked up his bags and then winked at Dolly. ''Sure would please me to take your picture one of these days, Miss Beavers, once I get enough money to buy another camera.''

''Well, thank you,'' Dolly said, blushing with pleasure. ''Maybe we. . . .''

''Get out of here, O'Grady!''

The young man jumped into the coach and scrambled down the aisle. But at the front door, he hesitated long enough to reach back and pluck one of Darby's bottles of champagne from its huge tub of ice.

Much later, Darby emptied their second bottle and propped his feet up on the ice tub as they neared the Summit of Donner Pass. Dolly was enfolded in his strong arms, her body stretched across the plush sofa.

''It's such a beautiful sight,'' she cooed, gazing down at the shimmering, sun-kissed Truckee River. ''It's like. . . .'' she pursed her lips together in a way that indicated she was into her deepest patterns of thought, ''. . . it's like a ribbon of silver that's leading us up to heaven.''

Darby stifled a groan. This woman was many things, but she definitely was not of a poetic bent. ''Yes,'' he lied, ''that's an apt description.''

She snuggled up tighter and drew a heart with their initials across the slightly fogged window. ''Tell me about the man who tried to sabotage this railroad.''

''Why?''

''Only because you hardly mentioned him in your last letter and that O'Grady brought up his name. It seems impossible that he almost killed you all after stealing that train at Summit Tunnel.''

Darby scowled and let his mind go back to that fateful day only a few months earlier when he'd managed, just barely, to lift an entire rail off of himself. He'd staggered out the eastern portal of the tunnel as Wesley Bryant and his men headed the train toward Reno.

It had taken a nearly superhuman effort to throw that flask of nitroglycerin at the receding railroad car. The resulting explosion had knocked him unconscious.

"Bryant almost succeeded in destroying all of us," Darby said quietly. "He was a brilliant man, and the most diabolical one I've ever encountered. What made it so strange was that he already had money. He was quite well off, from a good family, and he was considered very handsome."

She tweaked his jowls. "Not as handsome as you, Derby."

"Darby," he corrected. "I do wish you'd remember how that irritates me."

Dolly smiled wickedly. "Open one more bottle of champagne, pull the window shades, and let's talk about it."

"What about the scenery? The ribbon of silver leading up to heaven?"

She kissed him playfully and sighed. "Since we're almost there, I think it's time you unlocked the gates. Don't you?"

When the train whistled into Summit Tunnel, Darby and Dolly Beavers had forgotten time. They didn't notice the darkness because all the shades were pulled tight. *But* when the Central Pacific engineer barreled out the western portal into the sunlight and saw Mister Harvey Strobridge and his crew blocking his tracks just ahead, there was nothing to do but slam on the brakes.

And six cars behind the locomotive, two very startled passengers flew off the wide velvet couch and landed in the forgotten tub of icewater.

It was fortunate that the shrieking of steel drowned out the cries which exploded from their blue lips.

"My God!" Harvey Strobridge swore minutes later as he rushed into the coach. "What happened!"

The couple glared at him with such malevolence that the big Superintendent of Construction actually took a backward step. "Never mind," he said, "I don't think I want to know. Besides, Crocker wants to see you at once."

Darby, not trusting himself to speak, merely nodded. He shook the water from his clothes and tried to hold his temper and avoid the questioning look of amusement on Strobridge's face. A short time later he and Dolly emerged from the coach and O'Grady came to meet them from the one ahead.

"May I tag along?" the young man asked. "I swear I'll keep quiet."

Darby granted permission with an almost imperceptible nod.

The snows, which only two months before had been nearly forty feet deep in the pass, were now reduced to wind-blasted drifts. Here and there, in the ravines, under the trestles and trees where there was shade, it was still deep enough to bury a man. But it was nothing compared to what they had faced. At one time, they'd all lived in tunnels. The Chinese had built an extensive network of passageways and rooms under the drifts. All were melted away now.

They passed railroad construction and storage sheds, and farther on, the blacksmith shop and dining hall. Then they reached Crocker's dining and passenger cars, for which a special siding had been built.

"Go on in," Strobridge urged, "he's been waiting for you since we sent the telegram."

"What about my friends?"

"Take 'em in with you," the tall, one-eyed railroad builder said. "He'll tell them to leave if he's a mind to."

"Darby!"

Charles Crocker literally sprang from his desk chair and, if Darby hadn't been a powerful man, the sight of so large a mass launching itself at him would have been unnerving. Charles Crocker was huge and weighed nearly three hun-

22

dred pounds—most of it gone to fat. The man had a thick goatee sprouting from his determined chin. He was wearing a bright blue smoking jacket that accentuated his paleness.

"Darby, thank heaven you came. I . . . I'm afraid once again I must beg for your assistance."

"You need only *ask*, sir." He gestured toward Dolly. *"This* is the woman I told you about."

Crocker's eyes lost a trace of their worry and he nodded with appreciation. "You are even lovelier than Mister Buckingham promised."

That thawed Dolly out. She bowed slightly and flashed the railroad President her most dazzling smile. "How perfectly gallant you are to say such a thing. I. . . ."

"And this," Darby interrupted, fearing that the champagne might have unlocked her precious few inhibitions, "this is my . . . cousin, Mister Connor O'Grady."

Crocker didn't succeed in disguising his surprise. Except for the fact that they both wore suits and derby hats, there couldn't have been two more dissimilar figures. One was tall and slender, the other was built like a tree stump.

"Well, this is a pleasure, young man. Darby never told me about having a cousin."

"He didn't know," O'Grady said quietly. "I'm new in his life—and in the west, for that matter."

"What line of work are you in?" Crocker asked.

"I'm a reporter, sir."

Crocker's expression grew troubled. "Then I'm afraid I must ask you to leave us in private. You see, I must discuss some grave matters with Mister Buckingham. Perhaps you and Miss Beavers would enjoy going through that door into the dining car. I'm sure my Chinese cook will be happy to pour you a drink and take your orders for dinner."

"I'll have my usual too, sir," Darby said a little too quickly.

"Of course. Mister O'Grady, please tell Soo that Mister Buckingham will have a full ham glazed in oriental spices and brown sugar."

Darby was flattered that Crocker remembered. As the

other two filed out, however, he was eager to get to the source of the railroad President's anxiety. Whatever it was, it could be handled. After all, they'd teamed once before to beat the Sierras and Wesley Bryant's saboteurs.

He declined a brandy, and watched Crocker pour himself a double and sink back into a leather chair. "Darby, I scarcely know how to tell you what I must."

"Do it directly, sir. Do not mince words. We never have before."

"True." Crocker took a shuddering drink. "Please be seated."

The door swung open and Chen Yun, the leader of Crocker's army of Chinese laborers, entered the lavishly appointed passenger coach.

Darby strode over and enveloped his friend's hand and bowed in greeting.

Chen Yun received a nod from the railroad President, then reached into his tunic and retrieved a golden, bullet-pitted medallion.

Darby stared in disbelief. Chen Yun had given him this medallion when first they'd met, in reward for saving his life.

The medallion was a priceless art object handed down from generations in Chen Yun's family. Almost as large as the Chinaman's palm, it was beautifully carved in relief, with a picture of the sun shining over a peaked mountain beside which a lion rested. Darby turned it over. Once, this medal had saved his own life and the imprint of a rifle's bullet was impressed in the gold. Even so, it hadn't obliterated the image on the back side of the medallion, a slain deer around which a snake was entwined.

"Do you remember the story?" Chen Yun asked.

"I would never forget what you told me," Darby said evenly. "It is the legend of a young boy who journeyed up a mountain in search of God. The lion is a symbol of the courage he must possess to complete the journey."

"And the stag with serpent?"

"A reminder that he may become entwined in deceit

and self-ruin if his heart is weak as he begins his perilous journey."

Chen Yun nodded. His face was impassive, yet Darby knew he was immensely pleased that the legend was not forgotten.

"And now you must prepare for such a journey, my friend," Chen Yun told the writer.

"What are you talking about?" Darby looked questioningly over at Charles Crocker.

"Do you know where the medallion was recovered?"

Darby shook his head. Wesley Bryant had taken it from him only moments before Darby had thrown the nitroglycerin and blacked out. The Chinese must have located the stolen medallion somewhere near the explosion. It was miraculous that he had it back.

Crocker finished his brandy. "It was found in a San Francisco pawn shop."

"What! But that couldn't be!"

"But it was. One of Chen Yun's men saw it in the window. We just received it, and that's when I sent you the telegram."

"But. . . ."

Crocker held up his hand. "Let me finish," he said gravely. "I had other business in San Francisco. Do you remember all those stocks I said were taken from my safe by Wesley Bryant?"

"Yes." Darby felt a deep dread forming in the pit of his stomach. Crocker was leading him inexorably toward something he did not want to face.

"They've just begun to turn up, forged, of course."

"Do you know the thief's name?"

Crocker looked quickly away. "Tell him, Chen Yun."

The Chinaman's black eyes did not waver as they met those of the novelist and he said, "Mister Bryant *lives.*"

Darby's fingers snapped shut around the medallion like an animal trap. "Impossible!" he whispered.

"No, my friend, it is not. He has been seen. My people call him THE MAN OF TWO FACES."

"Two faces?" Darby felt stunned by the news, unable to believe what they were telling him. The last instant before he'd thrown the flask of nitroglycerin at the departing train, he'd seen Bryant shooting back at him from the rear coach. The explosion *had* to have killed him!

Crocker's words sliced through the confusion of his thoughts. "You were the only one of us outside the tunnel when the explosion detonated and knocked you unconscious. It must have hurled Bryant down into the ravine. Maybe he rolled for hundreds of feet down to the river. We don't know how, but he *did* survive."

The railroad President stood up and his voice was thick with hatred. "Somehow, he got away with our stocks and reached San Francisco. One side of his face is reported to be disfigured from the explosion. The other side was unscathed."

"Thus THE MAN OF TWO FACES," Darby said, with numb acceptance.

"Yes. He probably had to sell that medallion because it was all he had of value until he could get established. It bought him *time*, Darby, time to retrieve my stolen Central Pacific stocks and enough money to have them expertly forged and sent to eastern and European money capitals where they were cashed."

"How much?"

"Half a million, so far."

"My God! Can't you recall the stock?"

"Not," Crocker said softly, "without ruining the financial credibility of the entire Central Pacific Railroad and throwing myself and my partners into bankruptcy. And *that* would wipe out the savings which thousands of Americans have invested—on faith—in our company."

Darby swore. "How much more stock does he have?"

Crocker poured two more brandies. The neck of the decanter rattled along the lip of both glasses and his hand shook when he extended the drink to Darby. He'd grown old in a matter of hours.

"A million and a half, Mister Buckingham."

They emptied their glasses.

"And that's why you have to stop him *now.*"

"But, why me? I mean, I will help, sir, but. . . ."

"Don't you see? If word of this reaches Congress, or even the press, we are finished. It would cause a panic on the stock market."

The railroad President rested his hand on Darby's powerful shoulder to steady them both. *"You're* the man for it," he said thickly. "You alone understand how Bryant thinks and reacts. You were the only one who could trap him before. *Please* do it again!"

The writer couldn't bear to see the desperation in those eyes. So he nodded. "I'll find him," Darby Buckingham promised. "And this time, I'll make dead certain he is stopped permanently."

"He's gone underground, Darby, organized a network of smuggling and vice, and hired a vicious Chinese Tong to protect his interests and eliminate all opposition. Everyone fears him now, and getting cooperation will be nearly impossible. I can't even tell you how to proceed."

"Any idea as to the location of his headquarters?"

"No one knows. My own intelligence sources say he seems to be everywhere. One report is that he is in Sitka, Alaska, where he controls the Russian timber rights. Some say he lives in the bowels of San Francisco itself, while still others say he inhabits a sailing ship which sits in the harbor. We do know that he has already begun to deal in prostitution and slavery among the Chinese men and women he imports. I've heard he has gained almost complete control of the opium market."

"At least," Darby said, "he doesn't know I'm coming."

Crocker agreed. "If he did, you would be dead before you passed the city limits."

Darby believed him.

A few minutes later, when Darby stepped out into the forest to light a cigar and walk in solitude under the stars, he thought about how Wesley Bryant, once a handsome and brilliant man, in his arrogance and pride, would rot with hatred because of a facial disfigurement. One thing was certain: if Bryant ever had a chance to repay the Derby Man, he'd move mountains to exact a horrible vengeance. Darby paced thoughtfully between the tracks in silent contemplation. It wasn't like a Buckingham but, inside, wrapped deep under the layers of muscle, there now lay buried a kernel of fear.

Chapter 3

The crunch of boots on gravel sent him spinning around in the night. Darby's hand flew into his coat pocket and the derringer came out, pointing down the tracks. Not that he was any good at hitting anything with it, but there was always a first time.

"Who is it?"

He heard a sigh, then the sound of boots crunching forward, growing louder, until a tall, shadowy figure stood facing him.

"Connor? Connor O'Grady?"

"Yeah, it's me. I've got to talk with you, Darby."

He lowered the pistol. "I'm in no mood for surprises—or conversation."

"I'll bet you aren't. Not after what I overheard Crocker and the Chinaman tell you."

Darby's fists knotted at his sides. Damn this man! Cousin or no cousin, an eavesdropper had to be dealt with firmly. The writer strode forward and when O'Grady was a yard away, Darby's fist blistered an arc that cracked against the young Bostonian's jaw and sent him sprawling across the rails.

"Damn you! Get up and fight if you've any real Buckingham blood in your veins!"

O'Grady couldn't get up. He struggled, but Darby's blow had stunned him like so many others with its paralyzing force.

He yanked the redhead to his feet, cocking back his fist. "I ought to beat you bloody! Why did you do it? Mister Crocker took you in as my friend and you spied on us."

O'Grady shook himself free, then gingerly worked his jaw, testing it like a trap door. "I apologize. That's why I'm here now. No spy would confess to such a thing. And as for fighting you, if you ever hit me. . . ."

"Answer my question!"

"I wanted the story!" he shouted. "I'm not rich and famous like you are, Cousin Buckingham. This could be *my* chance to make a name."

"At what cost! You heard Crocker say that my only hope of trapping Bryant is the element of surprise. Were you going to rob me of even that much?"

"Will you quit shouting!" O'Grady yelled. "If that had been my plan, I wouldn't be here. I came to apologize and . . . and to ask you to let me help."

"Ha!" Darby cried in exasperation. "Don't be absurd. You'd get us both killed."

"Then you leave me no choice but to follow you to San Francisco and hunt this Bryant fellow alone."

"Are you mad?" Darby hissed. "Even *I* will be severely tested. I don't need you to sound the hunt. Muddy the dark and dangerous waters."

" 'Sound the hunt? Muddy the dark and dangerous waters'? Oh, for cripessakes! This is not one of your novels and I'm no armchair reader. The truth of it is you need a second pair of eyes to watch your back. I can be invaluable!"

O'Grady stuck out his hand. "I need a break," he said evenly. "I promise I'll willingly follow your orders. You've no choice, short of killing me."

"Hmm," Darby replied, "that is an attractive alternative at this moment."

But after long deliberation, he shook O'Grady's hand—because he was family and he *had* displayed some degree of initiative and fighting ability.

"What are we going to do about Miss Beavers?" O'Grady asked, his face splitting into a wide grin now that the issue was settled to his liking.

"We shall do nothing," Darby replied testily. *"I* shall

have to break the news that she must go back to Virginia City and wait for me.''

''Wise decision,'' O'Grady said. ''The lady would be exposed to our danger.''

''Of course. That is why she must return to Nevada.''

''Darby?''

''Yes.''

''Got any more of those Cuban cigars you smoke?''

He bit off a reply. The kid had brass.

Darby and Connor O'Grady took the train to San Francisco the very next morning. Dolly Beavers had wanted to go, but there'd been no choice. By the time morning had dawned on the Sierra passes, Darby had managed to convince her of his intent to send for her as quickly as possible.

It was a tearful farewell but, as the train rolled away, Darby knew she wasn't going to do some irrational thing like marry one of his old buffalo hunter friends.

The train barreled down the western slopes of the mighty Sierras, over the Butte Canyon Trestle and across the ragged face of Cape Horn, where the Chinese had blasted a roadbed. Down through the tremendous trench called Bloomer's Cut, where Harvey Strobridge, in his customary impatience, had lost his eye and almost his life to a faulty charge of dynamite. At Sacramento they took a stage, then a ferryboat into San Francisco.

In spite of the danger of his mission, Darby felt a fresh stir of excitement as they traversed the Bay to enter the city which had been transformed from a sleepy town into a roaring seaport by John Sutter's discovery of gold only two decades earlier. It was his understanding that, when the California gold rush finally ended, San Francisco had lapsed into a prolonged economic slump. Thousands had returned to their homes in the east. Then suddenly a bonanza was discovered on the Comstock and, once again, San Francisco came alive with the influx of fortune hunters and cargo bound for the deep mines just beyond the Sierras.

The city was everything he'd hoped it would be, and more. Despite his worries, the dime novelist felt its enchantment grip his spirit. The ocean air was clear and invigorating and he enjoyed the sight of thousands of seagulls wheeling in circles against the backdrop of an azure sky.

The bay itself was enormous and perfectly sheltered. Gone were the rotting carcasses of the old gold rush sailing vessels abandoned by the Forty-Niners, then cannibalized by the merchants for their lumber and fittings. Many of these ships had been towed to the shoreline and, eventually, had become part of the waterfront.

Portsmouth Square was still the place where a man with taste and money gravitated for excitement. The Square had once been the center of town—the Plaza, in Spanish and Mexican days. Now, it was the hub of the city with its plush hotels, restaurants, saloons and gambling halls, which attracted visitors from all over the world. It was a place where a European prince might be found tossing dice or watching a live animal show, while beside him the roughest of miners cavorted with a dance hall sweetheart.

They checked into the Parker House and Darby wasted no time in determining a plan of action. "We have to expose him and the only way we can do that is to start with his businesses—opium and Chinese slavery. You go down to the waterfront. Watch every ship that comes in. Ask questions, but be discreet. If Bryant suspects we're after him, our lives are in the gravest danger."

"What are you going to do?"

"I'll cover the financial institutions where forged Central Pacific stock must turn up. Banks, brokerage houses and that sort of thing. Also, I'll try to nose around in Chinatown. Chen Yun gave me the name of an old Chinaman who will help me if he can. He may be hard to find, but I should try."

"Chinatown is pretty big from what we saw on the way in. There're thousands of them and they all look the same to me."

"As we do to them," Darby replied cryptically. "Each

32

evening, we'll meet here in my room and compare notes. We haven't a lot of time. I don't know how long Mister Crocker can hold out, with Bryant's cashing in his stocks, but at the rate he's moving, time is valuable."

"Might help if you described the man," O'Grady said.

Darby quickly filled him in, then added, "but if he's as badly disfigured as we've been told, I doubt he'll let himself be seen by anyone but his closest accomplices."

"Maybe so, but at night I'll still keep an eye on some of these gambling halls," O'Grady said. "Money isn't any good to a man if he can't have fun spending it. And, who knows, I've a way with a poker deck."

"Watch out for yourself. These casinos are world famous for their ability to separate a man from his money."

O'Grady smiled. "Believe me, I've little or nothing to lose. See you tomorrow, and good luck."

"Same to you."

O'Grady nodded and left. He wasted no time in getting back to his room and scribbling several pages of detailed notes. Minutes later, he was in the hotel lobby asking for directions to the telegraph office. Notes in hand, he strode down toward the waterfront, trying to arrange the message he had in mind.

He felt some measure of guilt as he neared the office, but rationalized that he certainly wasn't going to betray Buckingham's secret. A story was a story and, unlike Darby, he was nearly broke. A tidbit of news would earn him expense money. He'd tell nothing which would jeopardize their search—only enough to earn him some working capital. San Francisco was no town in which to be broke. Besides, if he wanted information on a man like Bryant, it wasn't going to come free. A man got nothing for nothing.

He began to whistle. There were lots of pretty ladies in San Francisco and he appreciated the idea of a high old hunt through the intrigue of San Francisco's underworld. What more could an O'Grady ask for?

* * *

The telegraph office was in the process of being relocated, and it took him the better part of two hours to find its temporary quarters in the lobby of the Panama Steamship Company. There was a great deal of activity in the crowded outer office and the redhead was annoyed that he had to shout through the little grated window.

"I want to send a message to Mister Bolt, Editor of the Boston Globe."

The precise little telegraph operator adjusted his cap and grabbed a pencil. "Give me the message; I'll count the words and you must pay the charge *before* I transmit."

Damn, it was noisy! People crowded all about, yelling quotes for freight charges and haggling over a new shipment of east coast goods.

Someone jostled him roughly.

"Mister!" the telegrapher said sternly. "If you don't *know* the message, would you please step to the end of the line and let someone else take your place?"

"All right, dictate as follows," O'Grady growled.

From: Mister Connor O'Grady
To: Mister Bolt, Editor, Boston Globe

Have uncovered sensational new information. Am working with Mister Buckingham on confidential matter of possible national emergency.

Cannot reveal story now but will relay information as it unfolds. Magnitude of findings will shock nation. STOP.

Need expense money in advance. Please wire $300 now if interested. If do not hear from you in 24 hours, will contact New York papers. STOP

He expelled a deep breath. "That ought to do it."

The operator peered over his reading glasses with newfound respect, then counted the words. "That will be seven dollars and eighty-eight cents, Mister O'Grady."

He blinked. "I only have five. That's all the money I have until. . . ."

"Sir," the operator said, his coolness returning, "I'm sorry, but. . . ."

"Look. Ah, tell you what. Eliminate the entire middle paragraph. What'll that cost?"

"Four-forty. . . ." came the stiff reply.

"Fine," he said. "Here's four-fifty. Keep the change. I'll return tomorrow. Have my three hundred dollars ready."

Then, as the telegrapher cuttingly remarked that he'd be astounded if there was *any* reply, much less authorization for payment, O'Grady hurried away. He was confident he'd get the money. After all, once Bolt had been convinced that he and Darby Buckingham were on the closest of personal terms, he'd paid the stagecoach fare out west, hadn't he? Now the Editor had too much of the Boston Globe's money invested to back out. Besides, Connor O'Grady meant to give him his money's worth.

The impeccably dressed man who'd been intently studying the ship's manifest carefully jotted down the content of O'Grady's telegram. Then, with a bored look which concealed the excitement he felt welling up inside, he sauntered out of the building and, looking quite business-like, he followed the redhead.

It was only when he lost him in the flow of the crowd that his imperturbable exterior cracked and he swore angrily.

For several moments, he dashed about, peering up one street then another. How in the devil could he have lost a redheaded young fool wearing a green derby!

The man took a silver flask from his inside coat pocket and drank openly as the crowds flowed past.

Relax, he told himself. The information alone would command a good price at the local paper *but,* if he dared to risk his life, he might realize a hundred times that amount by taking it directly to The Man of Two Faces.

If he could get to him.

In the end, he *did* get to him—or at least he was on his way. He wore a black hood that stank of fish and his wrists

35

were bound. He was cold and very scared as they lowered him into the dinghy. Though he couldn't tell for sure, he knew it had to be nearly midnight.

For the hundredth time, he cursed himself for not taking the confidential information to the newspaper.

Greedy! That's what he was. And now, shivering in the fog, trying not to get sick as the little boat rocked against a strong incoming tide, he was scared witless. Fool! he ranted to himself. If the rumors he had heard about Bryant were true, the sharks might have an early breakfast.

The *Sea Witch* was a four-hundred-ton sailing vessel. Built nearly twenty years earlier in Norfolk, Virginia, she'd been the pride of an illustrious shipbuilding company which had since gone bankrupt because of its unwillingness to compromise on quality. The vessel lay apart from her waterlogged companions floating in the harbor. Her sleek contours were designed for maximum speed and her exceptionally tall masts held enough sail to outrun any pursuer on the west coast.

She had cannon, too, though they were hidden, as were nearly an acre of racing sails and the guards which patrolled her decks under the cover of night. Not even the most observant seaman would have detected that below her weathered, paint-cracked upper deck, there throbbed a command post as functionally efficient as any yet devised by a master criminal.

To all casual observers, the *Sea Witch* appeared to be only another of the abandoned ships left to sink or go aground after delivering its load of gold seekers.

And this was precisely the impression The Man of Two Faces had gone to great expense to achieve. Each night, a half dozen loads of supplies were dutifully ferried back and forth from the *Sea Witch*. Some were from arriving ships; others from restricted waterfront warehouses. They contained gold and silver, cocaine, Alaskan furs and, sometimes, beautiful Chinese women.

The informer felt the dinghy bang woodenly against the

copper hulled ship. He knew the sound well, for he'd come to California by sea as an argonaut himself.

"Get up," the voice ordered.

He leapt to his feet. The boat rocked violently and he had a horrible vision of being pitched blindly into the bay where he would thrash about until he drowned.

A knife slashed the bonds from his wrists and he was shoved against a rope ladder. "Climb smart, now!"

Though his fingers were numb from loss of circulation, he did. But, still hooded, he almost fell into the ocean when he touched the railing and grabbed for one last handhold that was not there.

Fingers dug into his coat and hauled him to the deck. Moments later, he was shoved down an almost vertical set of stairs. At the bottom, he fell heavily and lay still, gasping for oxygen, trying to suck it in through the coarse woven hood.

"Stand him up," an educated, almost bored-sounding voice instructed.

He stood and trembled.

"Remove the hood."

He felt the drawstrings about his neck being untied. A rush of air bathed his face and he smelled an exotic incense.

Then, he was unveiled. For an instant, his eyes would not focus. All seemed in darkness and he felt blind as they shoved him into a wooden chair.

"Do not look anywhere but straight ahead."

His eyes began to adjust to the room as he sat rigidly erect, not daring to move a muscle. Directly ahead, he saw a huge mirror, gold-framed and ceiling-high. Before it lay a magnificent oriental rug, the most intricately patterned he'd ever seen.

Then a woman, a Chinese goddess of a woman, entered his line of vision and, on the candlelit table before him, she poured what he supposed was tea into a bone china cup.

"Drink. Then you may begin to tell me all you know concerning the telegram."

He did as he was told, speaking into the mirror, aware that his face was illuminated and reflected for the speaker's benefit while he could see nothing but a dark shadow of facial outline.

"Did you follow the young man?"

"Yes, sir." He considered lying, rejected the idea as fatal. "But I lost him in the crowds."

"I see."

There was no judgment in the words. Only a registration of fact. The information seller felt relieved enough to add, "but he'll be back tomorrow. I . . . I could follow him then."

"And do what?" the voice asked sharply.

"And . . . and perhaps discover where this Mister Buckingham is. If . . . if that's who you want, I'll take you to him," he stammered.

"Generous of you to offer," the voice replied smoothly. "But that won't be necessary. I'll handle it from this point on."

His heart seemed   press up into his throat, beating wildly like a frightened bird's wing. "But Mister Bryant, I swear . . ."

"That will be all! Finish your tea."

The beautiful young Chinese girl's face was as void of emotion as that of an ivory figurine. She bent very near him to pour more tea. He was struck by her exquisite grace and suddenly realized that her eyes actually were a shade of lavender. His heart beat even faster. He blinked and her perfect, heart-shaped face began to go in and out of focus.

"No thank you, Miss. . . ." he said, having some trouble moving his tongue. "I. . . ."

Then, the heart which had been pressing up into his constricted throat burst, and he seemed to dive into the swirling lavender pools of death that were her oriental eyes.

Chapter 4

Connor O'Grady bounced jauntily into the lobby of the Panama Steamship Company and angled straight for the telegraph office. As before, there was a lively crowd of buyers and sellers, but he had to wait no more than five minutes before reaching the head of the line.

"Good afternoon!" he said, feeling buoyed by confidence.

"Oh," the man said, "it's you again."

"Of course. Hand it over, my friend."

"I'm not your friend, sir," he replied huffily as he shuffled through some papers on his desk. Finally, just when O'Grady felt the sweat beginning to bead across his forehead, the man plucked out an envelope.

"So," he crowed, "it's for three hundred dollars as requested!"

"He gave you an extra fifty," the telegraph operator said with a touch of bitterness.

O'Grady beamed. Now he'd have enough money to buy that fancy pair of Smith & Wesson .44's with their special quick-draw holsters. He'd seen them in the gunshop window yesterday and they were beautiful. He'd gone inside and heard the proud shopkeeper lovingly describe the weapons as using a center-fire cartridge with 25 grains of powder and a 218-grain bullet. None of that meant anything to him, but he liked the ivory handles and the way the guns balanced in his fist. He didn't know beans about firearms but, with the specially designed quick-draw holsters, he guessed he'd be able to hold his own among more experienced gunmen. He wished he had the time to go outside the city limits and practice drawing and firing, but there just wasn't any.

Anyway, he thought, with those .44's tied to his legs Wesley Bryant and his boys would now realize they were up against formidable odds.

He took the check and left the building. First, he'd go to a bank, then he'd buy those matched pistols. Wait until Darby saw him armed and ready for trouble!

"Good Heavens!" Darby blurted as the huge walnut armoire he grasped in his hands quivered overhead.

"My Lord!" O'Grady swore. "What are you doing down on the floor lifting that thing!"

Darby demonstrated his favorite exercise, his 22-inch biceps pumping, as he counted off ten more presses before gently setting the massive piece of furniture to rest.

"*You* should take up lifting," he said reprovingly, panting for air. "If you really do have Buckingham blood in your anemic veins, you ought to be ashamed of your lack of muscle."

O'Grady flexed a green goose egg and then drew back his jacket to reveal the .44's strapped to his side. "You supply the muscle, I'll handle things when the *real* trouble begins."

Darby stood up. He looked from the pistols to O'Grady's smiling face. "Why are you wearing them like that—with gunfighter's holsters? Don't you know you're just inviting trouble?"

"I'm quick."

"Yes, and also stupid. You'd be better off with a hide-out gun instead of those cannons."

The young Irishman was offended. "I'm going to learn to draw and fire. Maybe if you weren't so lousy with a six-shooter, you wouldn't have to lift all that weight."

"Forget it," Darby rumbled. "It's dinnertime. I've heard there's a small, basement restaurant nearby where the steaks are as big as a plate and thick as your wrist. Let's go."

"Are you buying?"

Darby indicated he would. They needed to work together. Besides, the young redhead looked half-fed and maybe
a few good meals would improve his thinking. O'Grady
didn't yet understand that the tied-down pistols on his
thigh were an invitation to a gunfight that would surely get
him killed. Darby hoped to change his mind before that
happened.

Darby waited impatiently. His black eyes kept creeping
over to the nearest table where a couple were eating with
obvious relish.

"Look at the *size* of those steaks!" Darby chortled
happily. "Didn't I tell you this was going to be a feast!"

O'Grady nodded. "Why did they have to put it in a
cellar?" He seemed to feel stifled in the subterranean
room. Darby tried to distract him as Connor looked nervously
toward the only entrance.

"Who cares," the writer demanded. "I wish they'd
hurry with our dinners."

Then, as if in answer to his prayer, he saw a waiter
coming with the food. Darby fidgeted with excitement. "I
haven't seen beef prepared to match this since I left New
York City!"

Suddenly, horribly, from a table near the steps leading
up to the door they all had entered, a man cried, "Fire!
There's a fire!"

Darby's platter of steak fell to the floor in the panic that
ensued. Men charged the stairway leading up to the door.

"It's locked!" a man shrieked as the mob surged
forward, trampling one another.

Darby stood up. He could smell the smoke now and the
hair on his back prickled with fear. "We must restore
order," he growled, "or we'll all die like trapped rats. Fire
one of those guns of yours into the air."

O'Grady yanked a pistol from his holster and ventilated
the ceiling. The shots froze the mad crowd and Darby
bullied forward yelling, "Step aside!"

Those who did not move quickly enough were rudely
shoved out of his path.

He could feel the heat from above. The air grew poisonous as he neared the doorway. His heart sank when he saw that the door was made of iron—a common fire prevention measure in San Francisco because of past tragedies.

Connor O'Grady grabbed the handles and cried out in pain as the flesh of his hands seared.

Darby ripped off his coat and wrapped it about the handles. The heat was intense. His body ran with sweat and smoke was steadily filtering around the thick doorway.

He reared back, pulling with all his strength. The iron door groaned, but held. He tried again and, this time, he braced his feet solidly against the doorjamb and, as his neck sank into his massive shoulders, a roar issued from his white lips. This time, the door bent. He *felt* it move.

He took a deep, tortured breath of air and the gases he inhaled choked him like a noose. One second the door was bending, the next he was dizzy and staggering as the room began to spin.

O'Grady caught him or he would have fallen. "Everyone get back!" he yelled.

But the panicked crowd did not move. They stood blocking the stairway, afraid to retreat from the only possible avenue of escape.

O'Grady's left-side .44 was still loaded and he went for it. The gun's hammer caught in the fold of his green vest and, in his excitement, he emptied several shots that ripped up steps between the legs of men below. They leapt back in mad retreat.

"Are you all right?" O'Grady asked, still supporting Darby as they moved down to safe air.

Darby fought to clear his head. His lungs burned and he felt like a vise had been clamped around his rib cage.

Above his head, the rafters erupted in flame and Darby knew their only chance to live was the possibility that, somehow, the flames would eat away around the hinges and he could tear away the iron door. But by then they might all be dead from smoke and gas.

42

His gaze fell on a forgotten and overturned bottle of champagne still fizzing across the table.

"That's it!" he shouted, pointing down at it.

Every man in the room swung around to see what he was staring at.

"That's what?" O'Grady yelled. "We've still got to try and get out of here. Getting drunk won't...."

"Don't you see? Maybe we can shake up the bottles and soak this side of the door frame, letting the opposite side burn. Then we might be able to tear it loose."

"That's crazy!" a man from below shouted in a furious voice.

"Have we anything to lose?" O'Grady bellowed. "Get more champagne. Empty the place! Let's go!"

The waiter dashed into the kitchen, directing several men to the wine cellar. Seconds later, they hauled out four cases of champagne.

"Open them up and put your thumbs over the tops. Then shake hell out of them and charge the stairway. Empty them at the door frame. Hurry!"

Never before in history had men opened bottles of champagne with more enthusiasm. Most took a long drink before they jammed a thumb into the bottleneck and charged the stairway.

Champagne erupted at the iron door, sizzled and stank, as the men fell back from the heat and others charged with fizzing bottles. Some tripped and shattered their bottles; others caught hot champagne and cinders in their eyes and emptied their bottle everywhere *but* at the doorway as they reeled blindly about in the smoke and steam.

It seemed crazy but at least they were doing *something* rather than resigning themselves to death. In spots all along the ceiling, flames began to lick their orange tongues through the planking. Then, an entire timber exploded. One end broke away and fell into their midst as men scattered. O'Grady yelled for help to douse it out.

He and Darby knew their time was all gone. In a few more minutes, the entire ceiling would bury them in flames.

Darby snatched a bottle from one man and emptied it on the door's handles, then he gripped them and threw every ounce of muscle he possessed into one gigantic effort.

The door frame split like a crack of lightning.

"Look!" someone bellowed. "He's tearing it from the hinges!"

A thin line of fire spurted through the crack and then, with a tremendous splintering of wood, the entire door ripped away.

Darby felt it tear free in his hands, saw flames burst through the opening and he reared backward, trying to use the door as a shield.

He was off balance, half-blinded and falling.

A fiery blast of heat and embers exploded over him like all the furnaces of hell and, as he crashed over backward, he felt crushed like a beetle under a Chinese laundryman's pressing iron.

Connor O'Grady wasn't powerful, but there was a deceptive hardness to his lean body. He grabbed the door and heaved it aside yelling, "Everyone grab a bottle and spray a path out of here. Go!"

They didn't have to be told again. With grim expressions, they emptied the last of the cases and, at a signal, the crowd charged the stairs as the familiar bells of the fire engine companies clanged in the night.

O'Grady managed to get Darby to his feet and hooked the writer's arm over his shoulder as the last of the diners surged by.

"Come on!" he urged as a section of roof caved in over by the kitchen, blasting flames at them. "We're getting out of here!"

Somehow they made it, and walked right into a blast of firehoses from the hand pumpers.

Volunteer firemen dashed into the charred remains of the upper floor to help O'Grady drag and half-carry the Derby Man out onto the street.

O'Grady looked into the eyes of a young man his own

age and saw fear. "Get him out of this part of town," the man said in a rushed voice. "The fire has jumped the alley and is burning free on three other buildings. It may get out of control."

"The block?"

"The whole city, man! It happened once before, on Christmas Eve of '49. They had to dynamite buildings to make firebreaks. The only hope we've got tonight is that the wind is down. Now get out of here!"

He raced off as others shouted orders and everything seemed in chaos. O'Grady glanced up to see flames leap to the rooftop of another building. The pitiful hand pumpers tried vainly to direct a stream of water to the fire but there wasn't enough pressure. All they could do was wet the walls.

A torch boy raced by, barely able to lead the way for a hand-pulled fire engine whose banner proclaimed the Knickerbocker Five. O'Grady saw the boy drop his torch, veer off sharply and fall to the curb gasping for air. Seconds later, he rose to his feet and staggered after his company.

A pack of dogs raced wildly down the street, running hard and silent for the distant hills.

O'Grady peered into the same darkness and quickly inspected Darby. He heaved a sigh of relief when he discovered there appeared to be no more damage than a sharp blow to the head.

It was time to go, as far and as fast as he could, before everything went up in flames. He tried to lift Darby again, but this time the adrenaline wasn't running as high and he barely managed to get him erect. Suddenly, out of the smoke, he saw a slender Chinese coming in his direction, pulling one of their familiar two-wheeled carts.

"Hey!" he yelled, running forward to grab the forked handles. "I'm sorry, but I'm going to have to take this!"

The Chinese looked into his face. He realized that it was a young woman and when she spoke, it was in perfect English. "Of course. I will help you."

O'Grady blinked in astonishment, then wheeled around

45

to grab Darby and pull him over to the cart. The girl helped him drape the writer across the seat. The cart groaned and sagged, but held.

"Let's go!"

They each grabbed one of the long shafts and began to pull the cart over the rough cobblestone street. They came to a hill and O'Grady almost died trying to drag the burden over its crest, but the Chinese girl seemed inexhaustible. When they reached the top, he halted, fighting for breath.

Behind him, he could see the building below and then he heard a roaring explosion and remembered—they would be dynamiting firebreaks again.

"All right," he wheezed, "it's all downhill now!"

They began to descend, too quickly, the weight of the cart prodding them forward. The girl yelled something he missed and then the cart began to pick up speed. He had to walk faster, then he broke into a jog, and then he was running, shouting at the girl. She fell aside and rolled as the cart swung around in a crazy half-circle and flipped in the street.

O'Grady lit heavily but managed to roll; he jumped up and rushed to Darby. The writer groaned.

"Are you alive?" Connor stammered.

His eyes fluttered open. "O'Grady?" he muttered.

"You *are* alive. Wake up, man!" He dropped Darby's head and rushed up to the girl. She was bruised and dazed but struggling to get up from where she'd come to a stop under a gas streetlamp.

O'Grady knelt and carefully turned her over to rest her head in his lap. "It's all right, little China girl. We're out of danger now . . . say, you are absolutely beautiful!"

The lamplight turned her face to gold. She struggled to rise, but seemed too weak. "Tell me, sir, will the fire reach my people in Chinatown?" she asked anxiously.

"Why . . . why, no. No, I don't imagine it will. Who . . . *what* are you? Some kind of angel of mercy?"

"I am Lee Ming. I was going to Chinatown to help if fire came."

"Your cart is busted to pieces," he said. "I am Connor

O'Grady. The man down below is going to be fine. He's my cousin, the famous Derby Man. He's also rich, and will buy you ten carts if you wish.''

She smiled then, and O'Grady knew she was the loveliest creature he'd ever seen.

She tried to get up but almost fell as he grabbed her.

"My ankle," she said in obvious pain, "I must have twisted it."

He lifted her into his arms. Under those baggy clothes, he discovered there was far more woman than he'd suspected.

"Mister O'Grady is *very* strong. And very kind to help Lee Ming."

"Oh," he said reverently, "it is Connor O'Grady and Mister Buckingham who are truly grateful."

She smiled demurely as he went down to Darby who was now standing erect, though unsteady. At one point, he saw the firelight dance off of her face and he stopped in his tracks.

"Your eyes," he whispered, "they're the most beautiful color I've ever seen. They're . . . lavender colored."

Lee Ming smiled and, in doing so, her beautiful face became heart-shaped.

Right then and there, Connor O'Grady knew he'd fallen in love one more time.

Chapter 5

Bryant knew the girl would return, because she was his slave. If anything was characteristic of a Chinese woman, it was strict obedience. In China, sons were important, because they carried on the family name and tradition. Daughters, however, were considered a misfortune, chattels to be married off or sold.

Bryant had visited China many times on journeys to establish his opium trade. The country was bitterly poor. The Manchu dynasty, which had ruled since the mid-seventeenth century, was layered with corruption. Between 1846 and 1850, floods had alternated with blistering droughts to create massive famines. Bandits ruled the countryside, and in the cities, never-ending, violent wars raged among the family networks.

The California Gold Rush had been almost propitious. Thousands of Chinese had fled their starving, war-torn country to come to America in search of Gum San—the land of the Golden Mountains. In villages throughout China, and in the city of Canton, stories were told and retold of the place where gold was to be found lying in the streets. The young men of China—hungry, weary of killing, had packed all their worldly possessions in a single bamboo basket and taken a boat to Hong Kong. There, the lucky, wealthier ones arranged with passage brokers to cross the Pacific Ocean. The price was high. Since most had no funds, they arranged to go on credit and work off the price of their tickets. By the time interest and expenses were added, the total fare often came to several hundred dollars.

They had come anyway. The luckier ones sailed on sleek Clipper ships and made the journey in two months. Others, less fortunate, had died by the hundreds in stinking cargo holds or gone down in unworthy old ships unequal to heavy seas.

Lee Ming and her brother had gotten only as far as Hong Kong. They were just children, but because of the young girl's beauty, they'd found employment in the city with a rich Chinese importer. His original intent, no doubt, had been to save the girl for his own pleasure. But, somewhere in the passage of time, and even before she was twelve, the little girl had completely won the old rogue's heart and become like a daughter to him. He'd lavished gifts on her, and provided her with a formal education and fine clothes. But then he had died and his jealous wife and daughters had vengefully sold Lee Ming and her brother to the highest bidder.

Bryant still considered it most fortunate that he'd been in Hong Kong the day of the auction. Lee Ming almost had been sold into the city's most exclusive prostitution ring. He hadn't even minded buying her brother and had immediately bonded him over to the Russians in Sitka.

All that seemed to have taken place quite some time ago, although, in truth, it had been less than five years. He'd taken Lee Ming as his mistress and she'd served him well, though it annoyed him at times to realize she'd never broken to his will. Bryant was certain that she hated him and would have run away long ago except that she feared for her brother's life.

"Master?" came the soft voice, followed by a tap on his door.

"Come in."

She entered the room and bowed gracefully.

"Did they burn, Lee Ming?"

"No, Master."

"Dammit!" he roared. "How could that be? Four city blocks were destroyed by the fire." He struggled to stifle his rage to think clearly. "What about Buckingham and O'Grady? Did you befriend them as I ordered?"

49

"Yes. They trust me now. They think I saved them from the flames."

He was shocked by the admission but he didn't strike her. "Maybe it's even better that they are alive for awhile. You can keep me informed of their every move. I'll know exactly how Crocker intends to stop me. Then, when I've had my amusement and finished selling out the stock, you can lead them to their deaths. Buckingham will never suspect you."

"Master!" she cried. "Please do not make me an instrument of death."

He sprang out of his chair, swept around his desk and came to tower over her. "You are *mine* and you will do as I will. I *am* your master."

Her eyes clashed with his own. "Then kill me, but I will not take the lives of your enemies."

He slapped her—hard. She fell at his feet and he resisted the urge to kick her for her disobedience.

"My enemies are *evil!*" he gritted. "The man you gave the poison to was a viper. These men, Buckingham and O'Grady, are worse."

He knelt beside her. "All right," he said, thumbing away blood from her lip, guilt sweeping over him. She was the only woman on earth who could make him feel remorseful.

"Look," he said, reaching out to unravel the queue from her long black hair so that he might see her differently. "I didn't mean to hit you. But . . . but until this big Alaskan deal is finished, you'll have to do exactly as I say. Understand?"

She nodded.

"You will not have to kill them, Lee Ming," he added quietly, as he tilted her face up to his own.

Tears of happiness welled from her eyes and he took her into his arms. This one was more than a mistress. That was dangerous, yet, if a man had only one weakness, what better one than his own slave girl?

He kissed her lips. "You must help me trap those who

would trap me. Is this too much to ask for all my kindnesses?''

"Oh no, Master!"

"Good," he said huskily. "I want you to go back to the city and build on their trust. Find out how they would hunt me. Do not listen to their lies or your mind will be poisoned. Do you understand?''

"Yes. And . . . and to do these things, must I sleep with your enemies?''

"No!" he choked, his fingers biting into her soft flesh.

"Then it will be very hard."

He chuckled and traced the line of her neck with a forefinger. My dear girl, he thought to himself, if you only knew the power of your own charms.

Darby Buckingham smoked his cigar and stared down from his window at the young couple as they exited the Parker House. Connor O'Grady looked like a kid with his first sweetheart. The young Irishman was entranced by the Chinese girl.

And who wouldn't be? Darby himself couldn't help but feel a tug of jealousy, even though Dolly Beavers was more than enough to match his energies. But she was in Virginia City and a man couldn't stop himself from at least appreciating beauty in another woman.

The girl had given them a remarkable account of the Chinese in San Francisco, how they lived, thought and survived. They were unlike any other race of immigrants who had come to America, because they did not arrive with even the slightest intention of remaining permanently.

The men were of a single mind. They'd left their wives in China to raise the children in anticipation of their eventual return. A single man saved his money in America, went back to China only long enough to father a boy-child, then he returned to Gum San once again in order to earn land money.

Lee Ming, it seemed, was one of the few unmarried Chinese women in San Francisco who had not been forced into prostitution. Bright and animated, she had a very good job in a waterfront shipping office.

The pair rounded a corner and disappeared, O'Grady's head bent low to hear the girl's voice. Today, he was going to ask her to help him listen for information about Bryant and perhaps even convince her Chinese friends in the office to help. O'Grady was certain she'd be eager to aid them. Darby wasn't quite so sure. Lee Ming seemed a little reluctant to discuss her personal circumstances but, after working side by side with the Chinese on the Central Pacific Railroad, he'd come to recognize their shyness.

He walked over to the bureau and retrieved his derringer from the top drawer, checked it and deposited the stubby little weapon in his coat pocket next to the telegram he'd received only yesterday. Another hundred thousand dollars worth of stolen stock certificates had surfaced in Canton. Bryant had to be stopped, and fast.

But how! Day after day of watching and questioning everyone he could think of had proved totally useless. Most had either never heard of Bryant—or else they were too afraid even to admit his existence.

The few that did were no help. Some claimed Bryant wore a mask, others swore his face had been restored by Oriental surgeons.

It wasn't until he'd finally managed to locate the old Chinaman Chen Yun had told him about that he began to think he might learn the truth about The Man of Two Faces.

The old fellow had sat against a well, his yellowed, parchment-like visage turned up toward the warming sun. "He is very evil. The Hip Yee's kill many people for him."

"But why?"

The Chinaman was a long time in answering; his words were tinged with bitterness. "He has great power. Bring tongs, slaves, opium and women."

"I see. Do you know where I can find him?"

"He come to Chinatown sometime in night. You wait."

"But where? There are hundreds of alleys and little shops!"

"You watch. He come soon."

Darby squatted beside the man. "You need money?"

"I like money."

"Here then. If The Man of Two Faces comes, you send boy to find The Derby Man at the Parker House."

The frail hand closed over the money, then crawled back into his pocket. "I send."

Darby stood up. "Good. Thank you."

The boy came two nights later and Darby raced immediately to find Bryant. But on his way, a pair of the Hip Yee Tong's members found him first.

They were the biggest Chinese Darby had ever seen in his life and he knew at once they were the infamous hatchetmen. Only they weren't swinging hatchets now. Instead, as they cornered and backed him to a wall, he saw that they were carrying a pair of five-foot-long ceremonial swords. And they looked sharp—rapiers with sharp points and razor edges. Fortunately, they were not light or fast-thrusting weapons. They were, instead, thick brutish blades with the severing power of a guillotine.

Darby made a grab for his derringer, but as the blades lifted, he knew he didn't have a prayer. So he did the only thing possible: he lunged at the nearest man. His shoulder buried itself in the hatchetman's stomach just as the other Chinese swung.

He heard a sound few men ever live to remember: it was the soft swish of tempered steel cutting air, not unlike a finger brushing silk, as it came downward.

Darby's legs were driving his man forward when, suddenly, the powerful Chinese body he gripped stiffened and, overhead, the man screamed as a blade bit into flesh.

Darby heard a grunt of shock and then he threw the dying man aside and leapt on the killer, smashing his face with vicious punches. The hatchetman staggered backward but would not fall; he threw his dangling sword aside and roared with pain and outrage. That's when Darby knew he was in for a battle.

Under the overhang of his massive brows, little eyes blinked twice, as if some cerebral circuitry had been jolted. Then, as Darby watched, the Chinaman roared with enough savagery to chill cannibals. Good sense told Darby to quit while he was still in one piece, but his fighting nature kept him rooted and waiting.

"All right," he gasped, kicking the dropped sword into the gutter. "No London Prize Ring Rules here. You want to kill me for The Man of Two Faces, then come on!"

He'd been hoping for some hint of name recognition, but he was disappointed. Then the warrior *did* come at him, with incredible speed for a man so heavy. One minute he was crouched like some monstrous toad; the next, his hands were going for Darby's throat as he hurled the writer against the wall.

Darby threw a forearm across his neck to deflect the grip while he buried his fist under the warrior's breastbone. This time, the Chinaman staggered as pain glazed his flat features. The hands sagged and he doubled as another blow sent him grunting into a half-spin.

"You had enough? I don't want to kill you. I'm a friend of the Chinese."

The hatchetman's answer was a guttural rumble in his barrel chest and then he spoke in harsh Chinese. Talk, it seemed, was useless.

The Chinaman leapt once more, only this time he was slower and his stiff fingers missed Darby's eyes and cracked against the wall where Darby had stood. He howled with pain.

Darby put him out of his misery with a final roundhouse punch which crashed just in front of the giant's ear.

He left Chinatown fast. Maybe the old man had betrayed him, but he didn't think so. More than likely, Bryant was heavily guarded and Darby had simply run into two of the guards before the others came running.

* * *

Darby was exhausted when he climbed the hotel stairs to his room. He wasn't sure if he was up for any more Chinese hatchetmen.

"Darby!"

He froze and peered intently into the dim hallway. "O'Grady?"

"Yeah. While you were gone, we had a messenger."

"Another one? What now?"

Connor O'Grady handed him a letter. "I saw the kid pushing it under your door. I tried to stop him but he got away. Better sit down before you read it."

Dear Mister Buckingham:

I believe it may be to our mutual advantage to have a discussion concerning your intentions—and mine.

I know the reason you are here and, should you think to decline my invitation, I will be compelled to inform the major newspapers of the world that Crocker's stock is worthless now that I have the bulk of it in my possession.

I would do this to destroy Crocker, whom I have always hated. Besides, my business operations bring in more revenue in a month than the value of the Central Pacific Railroad stock which I would be forced to dispose of. You see, I am more rich and powerful now than even The Big Four. It would, therefore, seem, Mister Buckingham, that you are working for the wrong side in this little drama. I offer you the chance to switch your alliance.

My reason for this offer is purely selfish, yet quite brilliant, as you have come to expect. Enter Chinatown at midnight tomorrow, alone and unarmed. I will find you on Dupont Street.

It is your only chance to live.

Sincerely,
W. Bryant

"It's a trap, for sure," O'Grady warned.

"I know. But maybe we can spring it and snare the man."

He lit a cigar and poured them both brandy. The vision

of the slain hatchetman was something that would go away only after a long time.

"It would be suicide to go unarmed," O'Grady said.

"Agreed. I'll take my derringer. Perhaps even buy one of those ridiculous pepperboxes."

"You're no gunman."

"Nor are you."

"No, but at least I can fill the air with bullets in a hell of a rush. That's why I'm coming."

"All right," Darby said with a tired grin, "I *could* use help. But you'll have to come up with a disguise. That red hair and green suit will stand out a mile away."

"Don't worry. I'll get Lee Ming to help me."

Darby frowned. "Maybe this time, you ought to leave her out of this. It could be dangerous."

O'Grady's face grew serious. "I'll think about it," he said finally. "Thing of it is, if lead starts flying and we have to dash for a hole, Lee Ming could be a really big help. Those are her people. If she asked, they might give us shelter."

"Don't count on it," Darby said cryptically. "I'm beginning to think Bryant has spies everywhere. I doubt if Lee Ming could trust anyone for certain."

The redhead patted his holsters and forced a confident smile. "Tomorrow, I'm going outside the city limits to practice with these. I'll be ready for anything by tomorrow night."

If the young man hadn't been so obviously sincere, Darby would have laughed outright. But it was no good to try and explain to Connor O'Grady that, out west, gunfighters spend *years* learning their trade, often to find their lives terminated by someone who'd learned it a shade better. The kid had grit, he had to admit, and with luck, maybe they'd both come through this thing tomorrow night in Chinatown.

But it was going to take luck and more than a hail of O'Grady's wild bullets to stop Bryant. The redhead hadn't seen a real Hip Yee hatchetman yet. Maybe that was just as well.

Chapter 6

Connor spent the better part of two hours and his remaining cash in the gunshop the next morning.

"Now, I ain't no gunhand, young feller, but I can give you a pointer or two."

"That's all I'm asking for, Bertram. I'll go out and get the hang of it this afternoon."

The bespectacled old man spat a stream of chewing tobacco into the spittoon. "Damn sure better spend more'n an afternoon, Bud. Those guns yore packing are just like signs on your hips telling the whole damn world yore a gunnie. Ain't you shot even a little?"

"No sir, but I'm exceptionally quick with either hand. Watch this."

Connor unloaded all six cartridges from one of his .44's. Then he tossed them up against the ceiling. As they fell, he easily plucked all of them out of the air before they'd fallen below his shoulder.

"So you can catch bullets," the gunsmith said drily. "That and a twenty-dollar gold piece will get you buried."

Connor was offended. "It's not easy. And I could probably do up to ten and not miss a one. Know anyone else who can say that? Huh?"

"Okay, I'm sorry," Bertram said. "So you got fast hands and good eyes. That's very important but it still ain't nearly enough to be packing those kind of guns."

"Then why'd you sell 'em to me?"

"This is a business, ain't it? Besides, I thought you knew something about shootin' irons. You want to sell me back those *used* pistols, I'll make you an offer."

57

"Offer!" Connor shouted. "I've never even fired them yet!"

Bertram shrugged as if it were out of his control. "Look, I'll show you how to draw and fire and then we'll be even. Fair enough?"

"Sure." He was still smarting over the "used gun" business, but at least the lesson wasn't going to cost him extra.

"First thing is that you've got to keep your body loose and your hands right under your gun butts. Then, when you make your draw, your hands ought to come pulling up in one smooth motion."

"I don't reach down and grab them?"

"Nope. You do that and your hands are changing direction from down to up. I'm telling you to sort of flip those .44's out of those special holsters while your thumbs drag back the hammers."

"Like this?" Before Bertram could stop him, Connor was sweeping both guns up. His thumbs missed the hammers the first time, but on their second pass caught them both and, before he quite realized it, the loaded gun exploded. The bullet drove a furrow the complete length of Bertram's workbench and ventilated a bean can full of cleaning solvent and rifle parts.

"Goddammit, boy! Put that thing away!"

Connor watched the can leaking onto the table. His ears were ringing and the smoke hung between them. "Whew!" he breathed, "the whole thing just happens *right now,* doesn't it!"

Bertram made him unload every cylinder and, even then, he acted nervous. He probably would have refused to say another word if Connor hadn't offered to buy a full box of cartridges to practice with later.

"All right, now we'll do it again only, this time, you don't try to kill me. Fair enough?"

"Yes, sir. Aren't you going to stop that can from leaking all over your bench?"

"It'll stop soon. Shut up and pay attention to me."

Connor nodded. It wasn't in his nature to let anyone talk

to him that way, but he'd excuse the old man because he seemed so damned excitable.

"Now, O'Grady, practice a couple of times, first with the right and then with the left."

"Why not both at once?"

Bertram seemed to swallow a chew of tobacco. His lined old face turned red and Connor was worried for a minute that the gunsmith was having difficulty breathing.

"You going to be all right?"

Bertram nodded and Connor felt relieved. He tensed, then drew again. This time, the left-hand gun caught on his vest and he dropped it on the floor.

"Dang!" he swore, scooping it up and inspecting it worriedly. "Did I hurt it? Bend anything?"

Bertram snatched the revolver away in disgust, then examined it carefully. "It's still all right," he said at last. "Bud, tell you what. These guns are too fine to learn with. I'll trade you some cash and a pair of old Navy Colts that'll hold up to that kind of treatment."

Connor was tempted. He'd been taking Lee Ming out to dinners and shows every night and his money was going fast. Besides, he was beginning to see that gunslinging was a little harder than he'd expected. Yet, what good would cash do him tonight if he had two old cap and ball pistols he couldn't quickly reload? Besides, those ivory handles were something to behold.

"Thanks anyway, but nope. I'll take that box of cartridges now."

"You through already?"

"Got anything else to show me?"

"Not likely," Bertram said in a troubled voice. "My advice, though, is that if you have to use those guns, get in real close."

"How close?"

Bertram shoved his little potbelly out until it touched Connor's belt buckle. Then he threw his head back and gazed up at the tall young redhead. "This close, Bud. That way, when you make your draw, you at least got an honest-to-God chance of beating someone to death!"

Connor laughed outright. The son-of-a-gun was joshing him! All of a sudden, he liked old Bertram a whole lot better. A man with a sense of humor had a lot going his way.

He paid for his cartridges and was going out the door when the gunsmith called, "Hey, Bud?"

"Yeah?"

"Where you going to shoot?"

"I'm not sure yet. I've rented a buggy. I thought I'd take a young lady out to the edge of town by those hills."

"Go south along the ocean. Pretty quick, you'll be out far enough to shoot on the beach. That way, if you drop those pieces, they won't be damaged falling in the sand."

"Why, thank you! That's a danged fine idea! But what'll I aim at?"

He thought it over. "If I was you, I'd shoot at the damned seagulls. Might as well. You and the girl being the only ones out there, they'll fly over and dump on you sure."

Conner blinked and nodded weakly. He hadn't thought of that. Lee Ming deserved a whole lot better but . . . but it *would* be good practice. Much more exciting than plinking away at bean cans.

Excitement. He hurried down the street toward the livery. Just being around the Derby Man made things happen. The man didn't yet realize what a good team they made. But he would. Right about midnight.

Darby tried not to look anxious as he followed O'Grady and Lee Ming into the foreign and exotic world of late-night Chinatown. The moment he'd entered this place, he'd felt an uneasiness, as though he were violating some taboo. It wasn't that the Chinese were dangerous or eager to do harm to a lone white man, because they were not. Most of them were simply suspicious and he could feel their eyes tracking him as he moved deeper into their city.

Fifty yards ahead, O'Grady was attracting even more attention—all of it adverse. When he and Lee Ming had emerged from a prearranged alley, Darby hadn't known whether to laugh or cry because O'Grady looked so ridiculous. His disguise was an abysmal failure by any standard. His hair poked out from under his little black cap in red tufts. His moustache was rubbed with charcoal and looked incredibly ratty with small bits and hunks stuck in it. He was way too tall to be Chinese and his pathetic attempt to stoop made him appear comical in his baggy tunic. His trousers reached far up his bony shanks.

As O'Grady shuffled further into Chinatown, people gathered to follow. Lee Ming was obviously begging them to go away, but their pointing fingers and childlike giggling only brought more to witness the clown act. Their subdued mirth turned into riotous laughter when O'Grady's queue, made of dyed rope, came unpinned from under his hat.

Darby groaned. It would have been far better if he'd come alone rather than be a part of this most amateurish charade. But he hadn't been able to dissuade O'Grady from going through with this pathetic attempt at subterfuge. What was even worse, if trouble did arise, Darby was genuinely afraid that O'Grady would yank out those two ivory-handled six-shooters of his and start blazing away. Some innocent Chinaman was sure to be hit and it would be their luck to be trampled to death in the ensuing riot.

All these fears had been crowding his mind since he had entered Chinatown from Dupont Street, slowly following O'Grady and Lee Ming. The streets were packed with men of all descriptions, ages and sizes. Most had shaven foreheads while the back part of their hair was gathered and woven into a long, braided queue. The Chinese visited among themselves, traded their exotic produce and haggled over displays of plucked chickens, turtle eggs and a thousand delicacies Darby could only wonder about.

He paused to watch a thin old man roll sticky opium paste around a long, black needle, then toast it over a flame. The sweetish odor reminded him of roasted peanuts and flowers. The paste became a brown, crystal-like substance and was transferred to the center of the man's pipe

61

bowl. Then as Darby watched in fascination, the old man put his shrunken lips to the bamboo stem, lit the pipe and sucked with one incredibly long intake of breath which completely consumed the drop of opium.

The Chinaman's eyelids fluttered like butterfly wings and his mouth opened in a vacant toothless grin as he held the smoke in his lungs until Darby thought he'd die. Then, slowly, the smoke wafted from his nostrils and he sagged to lie against a building and sleep his child's fantasies.

Darby hurried on, past the alleyway where pretty Chinese girls beckoned men with their hennaed fingernails. Their eyebrows were plucked but strikingly etched with charcoal; their faces were thickly dusted with rice powder and their lips were painted bright red.

Their dresses were, the writer thought, outlandishly colorful, gawdy to the extreme and quite revealing. But they had empty eyes and dead smiles. Small, delicate women, they were doomed slaves—sad little China dolls.

Like the girls, Chinatown's streets and buildings were brightly painted. The upper balconies were draped with flower-colored lamps and windchimes tinkled in the breeze; the night air was a pungent and rich mixture of sandalwood, incense, opium smoke, roast pork and dried fish.

"Excuse me, sir!"

Darby spun around on the balls of his feet and almost jumped on a white-haired old gentleman with a carved walking stick.

"Could you tell me which way to get out of here and back to Market Street? I'm afraid I got turned around and lost. None of these heathens speaks English. You don't know what a relief it is to find you, sir."

Though the night wasn't particularly warm, Darby mopped his brow before giving the man directions and hurrying after Lee Ming and Connor O'Grady.

Suddenly, necklaces of firecrackers sailed like garlands from the balcony above. They exploded between the narrow corridor of buildings in a tremendous cacophony. Chinamen dove for hiding under vending carts and into doorways. The air billowed with white smoke and, in an instant, the street was blanketed in a choking fog.

Darby shouted to Connor O'Grady and heard a dim reply, then the unmistakable rattle of gunfire. Choking on the smoke, he groped his way blindly forward until he was stopped by the blade of a hatchet shoved against his throat. Darby froze. Men pinioned his arms and found his hidden derringer. When he tried to resist, the hatchet blade was pressed against his skin and a trickle of blood rolled down to ruin his collar.

"Make no mistake, Chu would like nothing better than to avenge the Hip Yee Tong of a death. But first, I insist on talking with you," Bryant hissed. "Move quickly."

Darby could not see Bryant's face in the swirling smoke, but the voice was ominously familiar. He was propelled through a doorway into a dimly lit room. A candle flickered beside a smoldering pot of jasmine-scented incense.

"Sit down and put your hands on the table."

Darby weighed his chances of escape. There were none. Outside, he could hear loud voices speaking in English and Chinese. The gunfire and firecrackers were silenced. He peered at the gloomy interior and decided to do as he was told. Wesley Bryant's profile edged into the circle of candlelight and Darby stared back.

"So," Bryant hissed, "we meet once again, only this time, you are under my control."

"How did you escape?" Darby asked. "I threw that flask of nitroglycerin and saw it explode almost directly beneath your feet."

"I wasn't there when it landed. Actually, I was the only man who didn't go over the edge of that mountain trapped inside the train. The explosion caught me in midair. I felt as if I'd been hit by lightning. When I awakened it was dark and I was lodged in some rocks almost a hundred yards down the canyon wall. I won't bore you with the grisly details of how I escaped your searchers. I even managed to double back and retrieve the cache of railroad stocks."

"Thank you," Darby said. "If it's of any interest, I hold myself personally responsible for your continued existence. I consider it my greatest failure."

The profile smiled a half-smile, but even so, Darby could see how the undamaged side of Bryant's mouth was pulled lopsided.

"Do you wish to live?"

"Of course. If the price is not too high."

"The price for life can never be too steep."

"Yes, it can. But never mind that for now. What are your terms? We can, if I accept your offer, debate philosophy another time."

"I have your friend, Connor O'Grady."

"You are bluffing. He will not be as easy."

"Oh, yes. Even now, he is being overpowered as you were. He is my ace-in-the-hole, so to speak."

Darby's moustache twitched. "He's nothing to me."

"Fine, then I'll kill him because of Lee Ming."

"Lee Ming, you mean. . . ."

"My mistress. She does my bidding in all things. She is the reason you are here and also the reason that I know Connor O'Grady has been taken. But, for now, I need your journalistic abilities to ensure future American support when I become the Emperor of Alaska."

"Are you mad!" Darby roared, jumping up from the table as the flat of a hatchet crashed against his ear. He staggered and was jammed back down into his seat. His head swam with pain.

"You probably aren't aware of it, but I have, for several years, profited hugely from an exclusive right to sell Alaskan timber and ice."

"I've heard rumors about that," Darby said bitterly, "and also about your opium and slave trades with China."

"Yes, I am an entrepreneur. However, the Chinese are becoming sensitive to American protests and I'm convinced that, in a year or two, the Chinese will actually be excluded from entering this country."

"And there would go your slaves, not to mention a loss of opium sales."

"Exactly," Bryant said. "That is why I have decided that my real opportunities are in Alaska. Unfortunately, it is now evident that the Russians intend to sell Alaska to America."

Darby sat upright. This was news to him. "Why should the Russians sell? They've been here over a hundred years. In fact, in 1812, they even made a vainglorious attempt to colonize California at Fort Ross."

"The Russians have many reasons for wanting to be out of North America. Primary among them is their recent disastrous defeat in the Crimean War with England. They are broke and temporarily seized by an irrational fear of having Alaska invaded by England *and* America."

"Perhaps they are correct."

"Don't irritate me, Buckingham! I've sent envoys to St. Petersburg entreating Czar Alexander not to sell."

Darby didn't feel like it, but he grinned anyway. "But he won't listen to you. Not surprising, your position isn't exactly impartial, is it?"

"No. That's why I intend to buy it myself. Unfortunately, our Secretary of State, William Seward, has his own designs."

Darby shook his head. "Let me guess your problem," he said with no little amusement in spite of his predicament. "Wealthy as you are, you cannot outbid the United States of America."

"Precisely! That fool Seward has just asked President Johnson's cabinet for over seven million dollars—and they gave it to him!"

"Damn," the writer said with mock regret, "that *is* a lot of money."

"Yes, Buckingham. In a few more years, I'd have been able to swing it. God knows the Russians would rather sell to me than to the United States government. But they'll sell to the devil himself if he bids highest."

"Then what are you going to do? There is no way possible to influence this country's policies."

"Ah! But that is where you are badly mistaken! At this very moment, there's an American diplomatic envoy sailing north to enter into preliminary negotiations for the purchase of Alaska. He was sent by Seward with the President's permission."

Darby's heart began to pound. He swallowed drily. "And you mean to thwart those negotiations," he said with bitterness.

"Naturally." The voice grew taut with emotion. "I sail on the tide. Once I reach Sitka, I will set into motion a series of unfortunate events which will destroy any hope of an agreement. Czar Alexander will learn that a declaration of war has been issued against his country because of an unprovoked attack resulting in the death of the American diplomats. Naturally, the channels of communication will be sabotaged."

Darby's eyes burned. "And the Czar, having just suffered one defeat, will gladly sell Alaska to you for whatever he can get rather than lose it by force to the Americans."

"Very perceptive," Bryant said with a nod. "And *you* will help me keep it by writing to the most influential United States newspapers and Congressmen to the effect that I am a man of honor and decency—an American citizen who wishes only to be allowed to purchase his own wilderness."

"Never!"

"Then," the man shrugged, "you shall die while I will go about the business which awaits me in Sitka."

Darby's fingers gripped the table's edge so hard they turned white. He wanted to lunge at this madman and break his neck. But what if he failed? The American diplomats would be murdered and the entire course of history would be adversely affected.

He took a deep breath. He *had* to escape and that meant stalling for time. "Very well, in exchange for my life, I'll do as you ask."

"Excellent choice!" Bryant exclaimed passionately, twisting his head sideways.

And in that one split second, Darby saw the ruined half of Bryant's face. The mouth was torn and had reknit into a sardonic grin, and his eye was covered by a black patch.

Bryant's cheekbone was badly scarred and his hair was white now instead of black. He wasn't grotesque, but he sure wasn't handsome any longer.

Their eyes locked and Bryant, noting the twinge of surprise and shock on Darby's face, cried, "Yes! See what you did to me!"

Darby's fist shot out and he slapped the candle away as the room plunged into darkness. He threw himself from the chair and hit the floor rolling, then bounced erect and lunged at the doorway.

He missed it and saved his own life as a hatchet sliced empty air. Darby's shoulder struck a wall and momentum carried him through the flimsy structure. Then he sprawled into the street, got to his feet and began to run as bullets split the night.

"O'Grady!" he called, his legs and arms pumping for all they were worth. "O'Grady!"

There was no answer. Then, as he began to run and bullets started flying up the street, Darby remembered. Lee Ming. The trap. Connor O'Grady wouldn't be able to help anyone now.

He was gone.

Chapter 7

Connor O'Grady heard the fireworks exploding and his hands dipped to the guns at his sides. The right one came out fast, but he caught the hammer of the left one in his belt and almost shot himself as a bullet whined off the cobblestone street and ricocheted through a window.

"Darby!" he shouted as the smoke engulfed everything in sight. "Darby!"

He started to grope forward, but Lee Ming cried, "Please, Connor! Do not go in there. I beg of you to run before they come to kill you!"

"I've got to find him. Don't you see that? This was planned to separate us." He squeezed the revolvers. "But don't worry, with these babies nothing can. . . ."

"Kee Kow Yee!" came a frenzied chorus that made the Irishman's neck-hairs stand on end. Then, as he pushed Lee Ming behind him, the Chinese hatchetmen charged out of the swirling gunsmoke.

Connor's blood ran cold but his guns snapped up and he held his ground, then opened fire as a gust of ocean breeze pushed the smoke cloud over them all.

It was like shooting at ghosts! They howled and screamed and sliced at him from every direction as his new Smith & Wesson .44's barked in answer.

One hatchetman's cry took on a high-pitched sound. His weapon clattered to the street and he disappeared, wailing piteously. Bullets laced the air as Connor tried to find another elusive target.

"Ha! Ha!" he crowed, pivoting on the balls of his feet and waving the smoking guns. "Come on, you devils!"

He snapped off another shot that missed and then, just when the smoke was beginning to thin, he ran out of ammunition. The familiar sound of a gun's hammer smacking on an empty cartridge was well-known to the members of the Hip Yee Tong. One, a huge three-chinned fellow with close-set eyes and a flattened nose, grinned at his companions and then motioned them forward as he chopped his axe through the air in a fit of frenzy.

"Uh-oh," Connor said, shoving his empty guns into their holsters and grabbing Lee Ming, "let's get out of here!"

Up Dupont Street they ran with the hatchetmen in joyous pursuit. Connor's long legs were built for speed and, with fear prodding him, he'd have liked to have shaken the kinks out of his knees. Only trouble was, Lee Ming wasn't nearly his equal. She kept crying for him to let go of her and run on alone. He told her to save her breath and go faster.

They came to a steep hill and, halfway up, Lee Ming fell from sheer exhaustion.

He yanked her to her feet. "Come on. If we. . . ."

Connor's words died in his mouth. Lee Ming wasn't going to be able to outrun the pack that was so close behind them.

He pushed the girl aside and drew his empty guns one more time. His lips formed a thin smile as he cocked back both hammers. A *real* gunman might have been able to reload while at a dead run. Connor aimed the pistols point blank at the hatchetmen and yelled, "Come on and get it!"

They skidded to a terrified halt. Unsure, they glanced at each other, half crouching as though this might be a game of tag they could outdodge. Then, after a bit of shrill chatter, the same three-chinned one detached himself from the others. With great bluster, he hurled what must have been taunts at them. Lee Ming answered in kind and Connor was proud of her.

Then, the big hatchetman shook himself with rage, tore at his queue and made an awful roar. Connor knew he was working himself up to charge. "Stand back, Lee Ming," he said, "when I pull these triggers and they snap empty again, that one is going to go berserk. I'll try to hold them off while you get out of here."

Lee Ming shook her head violently. "No," she vowed, "I will not let you die!"

He chuckled nervously. "Honey, thanks, but unless you're hiding a cannon in your pocket, I think these boys have other plans."

She straightened, looked at the one advancing and began to speak in a hard, flat voice; the big man's hatchet slowly lowered. He frowned in puzzlement, then angrily gestured toward the bay. Again, Lee Ming spoke in that same tone which carried an unmistakable ring of authority.

The hatchetman seemed to wilt.

"My God!" Connor breathed. "What . . . how . . . what did you say?"

"I told him to let you live. That you would come peaceably and that your guns were empty."

"But why! Go where?"

"Connor," she said, unable to meet his eyes. "I have lied and tricked you from the very beginning. I . . . I told them what I tell you now. I am The Man of Two Faces' woman."

"No!" He didn't believe it! "Lee Ming. That's impossible."

Now she looked into his eyes, even as she slowly lifted her tunic and revealed to him the scar which had been burned into the flesh at her small waist.

Connor stared in a transfixed state as he gazed at the palm-sized, oblong-shaped brand which was split vertically, half seared and half untouched.

The Chinese, seeing it, lowered their hatchets.

"It is his mark. That of my Master. If any man touches me without his consent, they will die."

"But . . ." He couldn't believe this! "You mean he branded you like a horse or cow?"

"Yes. I am his slave. I know you cannot understand this but . . ."

70

"You're damned right, I can't!"

"I am sorry. I did not want to deceive you. And now . . ." She choked, trying to throttle the emotion in her voice. ". . . and now I will not see you murdered."

Connor backed up, his face a mask of revulsion. "So, that's how they've been keeping one step ahead of Darby and me! You're nothing but a spy!"

She brushed back tears. Her chin came up. "I love you, Connor O'Grady."

"Don't give me that!" he spat, his voice shaking with anger. "You just tell your friends here to let me and Darby go!"

"I can't."

"Why not!" he raged. "You just said you loved me. If there's any truth in you at all, tell 'em."

She rolled down the tunic to hide the scar of ownership, saying, "He has your friend and my brother. If you were to escape, he would kill us all. You must come."

"Oh no," he swore, "you've tricked me for the last time, pretty girl."

She bowed her head and whispered something in Chinese.

Connor just had time to reverse his grips on the pistols as the hatchetman lunged at him. He managed to lay a gunbutt right across three-chins' forehead and see him collapse before the others swarmed over him. As he was knocked to the street, he thought he heard Lee Ming cry out his name.

But then he remembered she was Bryant's slave. Even more, he remembered the brand. The flat of a hatchet blade drowned out the sound of her voice. And, in his bitterness of betrayal, Connor O'Grady was glad.

He awoke in a haze of crimson pain and only when he heard the girl's voice did Connor remember who he was and what had happened.

"Master, I beg you not to kill this man."

A laugh. The kind that chills. "My dear, I have no intention of killing him with Buckingham running loose.

He is now my insurance. But tell me, why do you care what happens to this fool?''

She remained silent.

"Answer me!"

"He . . . he is a good man. Very brave."

"And?"

"I love him," she said so softly that Connor was not certain he'd really heard the admission.

Flesh slapped flesh with a sharp, popping sound and Connor heard glassware crash to the floor.

"You fool! You stupid, ungrateful wench! I ought to sell you to the Fat Pig in Shanghai. And I could, you know. He has an eye for you and has offered me ten times your value."

"Yes, if that is your wish, but please do not kill this man or have the Russians. . . .''

Again Connor heard the striking of flesh, then the sound of Lee Ming's body hitting the floor. Connor slowly tensed and tried to drag air deep into his lungs so that it might clear his head and give him the strength to rise against the one whom he now understood was Bryant himself.

"Get up, Lee Ming!"

Connor heard quick footsteps, a cry of pain from the girl, then Bryant's voice. "I said, get up!"

Connor's eyes snapped open and, less than six feet away, he saw Bryant twisting the Chinese girl's arm as he tried to yank her erect.

"Damn. . . ."

He gathered himself and, not yet trusting his legs, managed to lunge at Bryant's ankles. His grip was strong from all his years of cleaning stalls, currying horses and handling the lines.

Bryant barked in surprise, then swore as he twisted around on one leg. Connor yanked the foot up against his cheek and rolled hard as the man cried out in pain and fell.

Connor was still weak from the hatchet blow, yet he knew there would be no second chance if he lost this fight. He lashed out with a boot and caught Bryant trying to rise.

Then he jumped on the man and tried to take his head off with a volley of punches.

Bryant twisted and threw him off, then came flying back with his well-manicured fingernails jutting stiffly toward the eyes.

Connor averted his face and the nails furrowed flesh across his cheek. He struck back and managed to connect with the jaw, but the man shook off the punishment and drove his own fist in hard. They grappled desperately on the floor, rolling and slashing, kicking and gouging without quarter.

Then Bryant managed to get a choke-hold and, despite everything O'Grady could do, his strength was not great enough to break free as the heavier man bore down with all his weight.

He was beginning to weaken when Lee Ming, her jaw set with grim resolution, grabbed a huge antique vase and smashed her master into insensibility.

The talons at his throat spasmed and then Connor's lungs began to bellow with fresh air as The Man of Two Faces sagged, then crumpled unconscious to the floor.

Lee Ming was at his side in an instant. "Connor!" she whispered.

He crushed her into his arms and said in a shaky voice, "You're square now, girl. I don't know how you got into a mess like this, but I aim to take you out of it."

She helped him to stand, but his legs shuddered like reeds. "Just a minute," he said thickly.

"We must hurry! When he awakes, he will kill us both."

Connor shook his head, trying to stop the bright lights from blinking on and off behind his eyes. "Where are we?"

"On a ship. We are about to sail."

"Where to?"

"Alaska."

He groaned. Tried to think. Maybe they could sneak up to the main deck. Somehow get a boat. . . . No, he thought, they'd never get away with it undetected. Then he remembered something else.

"The stocks, do you know where he keeps those stolen Central Pacific Railroad stocks?"

"What are stocks?" she asked. "Connor, we have to get away from here!"

"I'm not leaving here without those stocks," Connor said. "If we can throw them in the bay, then he's lost. They're the reason Darby Buckingham and I came to San Francisco. This is my chance to be a hero. Show Darby I'm equal to anything."

His green eyes darted around the room. "Where does he keep his money?"

"There is a safe in the next room."

"Show me."

It was hidden in the wardrobe behind Bryant's clothes. One look at its mass told Connor he was out of luck.

"Dang! I don't suppose you know the combination?"

"No one does, except him."

Connor pounded his fists together. All his natural instincts told him to grab Lee Ming and try to get to the top deck. Once there, they could take their chances in the water. He was a strong swimmer and could help the girl reach shore. But that would let Bryant escape with the stocks. Connor shook his head in stubborn silence. There'd never be a better chance than this.

"Darby Buckingham wouldn't leave without those stocks," he said after a long pause. "So I guess I can't either."

Connor strode back into the salon and knelt beside Bryant. He frisked the man and found a derringer up the sleeve of his jacket, and a hideout gun under his belt. When he was certain that Bryant was disarmed, he roughly shook him awake, then hauled him to his feet.

"You're going to open the safe for us. Move!"

Bryant staggered through the doorway, shaking his head. When he saw Lee Ming, he hesitated for a long moment, then said, "You made a very serious mistake in hitting me. Very serious. It may yet cost you your life, as well as your brother's."

"Just open the safe, dammit!"

Bryant knelt heavily and then he began to work the combination.

Twice he tried the handle and failed, and after the second attempt, Connor poked the gun in his back. "You're stalling and if anyone comes inside now, I'll kill you first. So open it and let's not play any more childish games."

Seconds later, they heard the tumblers fall into position. "Pull it open nice and easy, then step back slowly."

Connor glanced inside but his gun never strayed from Bryant. "There's a basketful of papers in there. Which are the stocks?"

"Lowest shelf."

He grabbed a handful and made certain he wasn't being tricked. He'd never bought or sold stocks, but these looked genuine. Printed on expensive paper, each certificate had the words "Central Pacific Railroad" stamped in bold letters across the top.

"Lee Ming, I'll need a sack for these."

"I will find one."

When she left, Bryant said, "Don't be a fool, O'Grady. There's no way you can escape. This ship is a fortress. You won't even make it to the railing. Be smart. Give up and I'll see you're rewarded."

"I'll bet, like the way you tried to reward Darby Buckingham a few hours ago."

Bryant flushed with anger. "He was lucky. But his luck has nearly run out. Even now, the tongs are searching for him. There is no chance that he will escape. What I'm doing now is offering you money, the girl *and* your life. Do you really think you can refuse such an offer?"

"Can't afford not to," he said easily. "My health just wouldn't stand up to making a deal with you."

Bryant sighed with exasperation and made a greatly exaggerated show of patience. "Look, O'Grady, those stocks are worth a fortune and I'll give them to you outright."

Connor shrugged indifferently. "That's no deal. I can

have them anyway." He took a sack from Lee Ming and shoved it at Bryant saying, "Fill it."

"It isn't going to work."

"Why not?"

"Because Lee Ming knows I'll have her brother executed if she goes through with this."

One look at her told Connor that Bryant knew what he was talking about. He smiled at the girl, hoping to let her know he wouldn't allow that to happen. "With this money, I'm sure I can buy half of Alaska, let alone her brother's life."

"Wrong again. You see, the Russians deal only in hard currency. These stocks are worthless to them, and without my connections, there is no way you can sell them for anything even approaching their true value."

"Mmm." Connor smiled. "I sure appreciate your telling me all this. Guess there's no choice now but to take you along."

"Are you crazy!" Bryant hissed. "My men aren't blind. They'll know in a moment that I am being forced at gunpoint."

"Lee Ming," he said, "We've got no choice except this one. Are you with me?"

"Of course."

"Good. If his men open fire, you jump overboard and I'll follow."

"As you say. But . . . but if something happened to you . . ."

He pressed a forefinger across her lips. "Nothing will. Let's go."

They went up the steps, Bryant in front with a gun at his back and Lee Ming close behind. When they reached the open deck, Connor saw that it was almost daybreak and there was a thin fog drifting across the water. If they could get into a boat, they'd be concealed in the mist.

"Order a boat."

Bryant shrugged, then cupped his hands around his mouth and yelled for the duty watch to fall in on deck. Almost at once, a trio of sailors came surging up from below and Connor heard several more running back from the bow.

"There're too many! We only needed one," he rasped.

Bryant coolly ignored him and the gun as his crew assembled. "Listen up. As you can see, I am being held at gunpoint."

Connor threw his arm up and locked it around Bryant's neck. "Damn you. I'm not bluffing!"

"Nor am I," the Captain choked. "Men, count to ten. If I am not freed, kill Lee Ming!"

Connor watched in helpless fascination as each of the sailors produced weapons, then aimed them at Lee Ming's head.

"They wouldn't!"

But, even as he said those words, they began to count. "One . . . two . . . three. . . ."

"Make them stop!" he gritted, shoving the gun viciously into the man's back.

". . . Four. . . ."

Connor's eyes darted wildly to the girl. "Jump!" he cried.

"If she moves, shoot!"

For a moment, nothing happened, then the count resumed. ". . . Five . . . six . . . seven. . . ."

"Bryant, call them off or I'll shoot!"

"Eight . . . nine. . . ."

He was beaten. He hurled his gun to the deck saying, "I should have known better than to call the bluff of a madman. We'd all have died."

Bryant retrieved his gun. "Yes, we would have. But, if I'd let you pull this off, once my associates heard of it, my life would have been forfeited anyway. Besides, I never bluff, Mister O'Grady. One bluffs only to strengthen a position of weakness. I have no weaknesses."

He pivoted to his crew. "You three, take this man down to the cell where we chain the troublesome slaves."

"Yes, sir."

"I'll take those stocks now, Mister O'Grady."

He tried to jump away and fling the sack overboard, but

they were on him too quickly. Bryant watched with an expression of tolerant amusement which died only when his eye came to rest on the girl.

"Lee Ming," he said in a quiet voice, "you have betrayed me."

"Yes, Master."

"You know that the penalty for betrayal is death."

"Yes."

"No!" Connor swore, fighting to break away as they pinioned his arms.

Bryant seemed not to notice the disturbance. His disfigured face was sad now. "You have been a great disappointment to me."

"Do not kill my brother or this man, I beg of you."

"Beg?" He laughed. "I didn't know you understood the meaning of the word. Oh, you've always obeyed. But not once, in all the time we've known each other, have you begged. I should like to hear this new talent you profess."

He squeezed her arm until the pain rose into her eyes. "Come, my dear," he hissed, "you may yet live awhile longer."

Connor broke away for a second and threw himself at the twisted madman. He got in one punch before they beat him to the deck and threw him into the hold.

The last thing he saw before he fell was the sun rising and suddenly washing Lee Ming's face with gold.

He remembered that vision as she was jerked from her feet by The Man of Two Faces. It was probably the last picture of beauty he'd ever see.

Chapter 8

They were after him. He knew that, although he could not say exactly why. Maybe it was because he understood Wesley Bryant, how his mind worked. Right now, Bryant would be hurrying to the waterfront with Connor O'Grady and Lee Ming as his hostages.

It would take a small army to keep the brilliant criminal from reaching his ship and sailing for what he viewed to be his glorious destiny in Sitka, Alaska. Bryant would be surrounded by the network of evil men who depended upon him for their profit and pleasures.

Still, Darby knew he must try. It was dark as the writer sprinted from one alley to another, constantly watching out for the infamous Hip Yee Tong who would now be hunting him. His single advantage lay in the knowledge that Bryant would be heading toward the bay and fleeing by ship. It was also his greatest disadvantage, because the Chinese hatchetmen would be ready to intercept him near the waterfront.

The streets were nearly empty at this predawn hour. Each time Darby moved, he felt as if a thousand eyes watched him. Yet move he did, though only through the alleys and side streets, where cats fought and screamed and the odor of decaying garbage filled the air.

A block over, he heard a noise, followed by footsteps. Darby cursed his own helplessness. He groped along the alleyway until his fingers encountered an empty liquor bottle. He balanced it carefully in his hand. It was no match for a hatchet—but it was better than nothing. Darby waited, then finally relaxed as the footsteps receded into the night. When he was certain no one waited in ambush, he hurried from the alley and continued toward the San Francisco Bay.

He passed a dimly lit police station and was sorely tempted to seek its protection, perhaps even try to get help. But after several minutes of deliberation, he was forced to reject the idea. He would only squander precious minutes. The policemen on duty wouldn't be sufficient to stop Bryant—even if they did believe his story. They might even try to forcibly detain him for further questioning while Bryant escaped. He simply could not take that chance. Reluctantly, he slipped past the station house and continued on alone.

Darby leaned against a brick building and surveyed the next alleyway. It was slow going in the darkness but, if trapped, at least the inability to see would help to even the odds. He dashed across the street and continued downhill toward the bay. Every yard he gained brought him nearer to danger of a showdown and all he held was a stupid bottle. Blast! For one of the few times in his life, he felt almost helpless.

He was nearly to the waterfront now. He could smell the tang of the ocean and the rotting seaweed, and heard the gentle slapping of water against the piers. Darby could also sense a change in the area. It was rougher—seedy and mean-looking. He saw a few men now, drunks mostly, some asleep outside the waterfront saloons, gambling halls, tattoo parlors and clip joints which were notorious for their violence and corruption. Only a fool or a desperate man entered this area at night alone.

Darby was a desperate man. He eyed the sailors and wondered if he might find others desperate enough to fight the hatchetmen for a price. Perhaps, failing that, he could at least obtain weapons.

He pulled out his wallet. "Blast," he muttered again. He had only two hundred dollars and, in this town, that was no fortune. Still, it was worth a try, so he eased forward until he reached a brightly lit street corner just above the waterfront. Darby hugged the shadows and his eyes swept the length of the waterfront dives. Only one, *The Captain's Place*, exhibited any real life. Though the night was chill, its front door was ajar and tobacco smoke filtered out in a stream. He could see moving shapes inside. A lot of them. Bursts of riotous laughter and then the sharp cry of a woman told him that, even at this hour, a party was in full swing.

Off to Darby's right, not forty yards away, a small dog began to bark as it flew into the street with its back-hair on end. Darby tensed. He was still a long run to *The Captain's Place* and he held no illusions as to his foot speed. He was a fighter, not a runner. The dog kept barking at something. Then, out of the shadows, Darby heard a soothing voice call enticingly to the dog. Something bounced in the street and the dog stopped barking; then, after suspiciously sniffing the object, gobbled it down.

Its tail wagged nervously. Darby heard the dog whine softly as the voice seemed to draw it step by tentative step back toward the shadows.

Then, so quickly that he was certain his eyes deceived him, the writer saw a huge outline leap into the street and the dog yelped as it vanished. The yelp ended so abruptly that Darby's own back-hair rose. He swallowed and his moustache twitched almost like the whiskers of a great cat which senses peril.

Darby gripped the bottle tighter. He was going to have to run soon. Daylight was fast approaching. He tensed and, just as he was about to go, three Chinese raced from the shadow and then disappeared among the black pilings near the saloon.

"Blast!" he cursed softly. Every minute he waited, the noose tightened. They knew his only hope of buying assistance or finding refuge was here. Even the Hip Yees would not dare to take on an entire saloon, because public reaction and retribution would follow immediately. Those tong members who survived would be hunted down and hanged without delay.

Darby kicked off his round-toed dress shoes, knowing it wouldn't help much. Then, just for good measure, he shucked his jacket, removed his derby and unbuttoned his vest.

"Well, Buckingham," he gritted, shoving a cigar between his teeth. "In a few more minutes, it will be daylight and you'll have no chance at all. Make a race out of it!"

With those words, he charged forward, hoping to catch them by surprise and gain precious yards.

But they were very alert. Before he'd taken a dozen strides, packs of them were angling in from both sides. He thought of yelling for help. He hadn't the time nor the breath to spare. Short, powerful legs churning, head down and lungs sucking in great whoops of air, he kept on a straight-line course for that open doorway, stretching for every yard he could before they intercepted him as surely they must. Connor O'Grady would have made it, but the Derby Man did not. The fastest Hip Yee raised his weapon and Darby clouted him right in the teeth. He went down with his hatchet and a pile of his friends tripped over his sprawling body.

Another man slashed at his shoulder, but Darby buried him with a looping left to the neck. He was almost there, dammit!

Angry Chinese oaths filled the street, but Darby was listening to the running feet which grew louder.

"Help!" he roared, feeling his legs start to weaken.

Two drunks staggered into the open doorway. Darby had just a glimpse of their shocked faces as he barreled forward. If they were seeing double, it must have looked like an attack by the Chinese army because both men did quick little steps and let out cries of alarm as they fell back inside, grappling to slam the door.

"No!" Darby yelled as he ducked another hatchet swing and flattened a runner. "No, dammit!"

Another hatchet whirred by his ear and spun end over end through the doorway. Shouting erupted, then the door swung closed as Darby, in his final effort, lowered his massive shoulder and hit it full tilt, ripping it completely off the hinges as he drove headlong into the saloon with the Chinese literally climbing up his back.

Darby rolled under the door and prayed it was stout as a howling began and hatchet blades thudded into the wood. This was met with a volley of gunfire which would have done credit to a full platoon of the United States Cavalry. Maybe it was cowardly but, as the battle raged over him, Darby hugged the door like a security blanket. It sounded like one hell of a fight!

When the shooting and screeching finally died to a few whimpers, groans and curses, Darby peeked out from under the door to lock eyes with a huge man with the wildest shock of hair imaginable. He was drinking rum, puffing on a stogie and cleaning his teeth with the point of a long curved knive. The man winked conspiratorially, ran his thick fingers through an equally wild cluster of matted beard and said, "Well, matey, I got to give you credit for knowing how to liven up a party. Now . . . who the hell you be?"

Darby shoved the door aside. There was a hatchet buried in it and big hunks of wood were torn out. It made him realize how fortunate he was to be in one piece.

He stood up slowly and, in a glance his eyes took in the entire saloon—or what was left of it. Busted tables, splintered chairs, three or four dead Hip Yees and several sailors with nasty cuts.

Brushing filthy sawdust from his clothes, Darby introduced himself to the big man and added, "I'm more than grateful for your assistance. It was gallant."

"Gallant? You gave us little choice, though it turned out well enough. I never seen Chinese so het up to slice a man. Like a damn Oregon woodchopping contest the way they took to that door."

He spat tobacco and puffed faster. "You owe me, mate, for slicing up a few of my boys. I'm Captain Clapper and these are the finest men ever to go out in a whaleboat. Right, men?"

"Yeah. Yeah," they all grunted, staring at him with a mixture of curiosity and contempt.

Darby shifted uneasily. He felt very out-of-place without his shoes and coat. His appearance was always deceptive to those who did not realize that underneath his outside layer of fat there was a mountain of muscle. Besides, he reflected with no little embarrassment, he hadn't exactly distinguished himself in the battle.

He cleared his throat. "I am both grateful and sorry for the injuries; I'd like to buy the drinks as long as you all care to indulge." Then, to show his sincerity, he reached into his wallet and counted out fifty dollars.

"Well now, mate," Clapper said, jabbing the knife excitedly into the air, "that's the kind of thanks we like to hear. Right, boys?"

"Yeah. Yeah," they all grunted once more.

"You'll be drinking with us, Buckingham."

It was a statement. And, as frantic as Darby was to leave, he agreed to stay for a round and to propose to Clapper a deal if he'd help him thwart Bryant's escape on the next tide.

As the bartender poured, Darby studied Clapper and his men. One look at them made it clear that they were hard cases whose only loyalty would be to the man who could pay the highest price. Darby suspected Clapper himself was the worst of them and, if he sought the whaling captain's help, he'd better not let down his guard or he'd be robbed and disposed of without hesitation.

"To your health, mate," Captain Clapper toasted, "and to whatever adventures a man can find in this dreary life."

The man drank his rum neat, but Darby almost gagged on the foul-tasting brew.

"Another then!" the Captain bellowed as his men slammed their glasses down and chanted, "Yeah. Yeah."

Darby waved him off. Time was wasting and, even now, Bryant might be pulling anchor. It was time to get to the point. "Captain, at this very minute, two friends of mine are being shanghaied to Alaska. I can see that you and your men are stouthearted and the kind who enjoy a good scrape."

"For a price, mate. Flattery buys no rum."

"Of course. I'm glad you come right to the point, because I am prepared to reward you handsomely should we prove successful in the rescue of my friends and the capture of my enemy."

"Let's see your money."

Darby hedged. "Well, actually, I have very little on my person. I would have to go to the bank and draw on my line of credit. You see, I'm the leading dime novelist for a very prominent New York publisher. His name is J. Franklin Warner and he has opened a substantial line of credit against my royalties upon which. . . ."

"Stow it, mate!" Clapper growled, "I don't understand nothing except what I can see, feel or swill. No money, no deal."

Darby reached into his wallet and counted out every cent he had. "Here's one hundred and fifty dollars cash advance. You help me and I'll pay you another two thousand."

The Captain's bushy eyebrows shot up. "Well," he said, "this enemy of your'n must be pretty important for that kind of money. Who is he?"

"His name is Wesley Bryant."

"Never heard of him."

"In Chinatown, he's known as The Man of Two Faces."

Clapper snatched up the bottle of rum and drank it straight. When he lowered his head, he graveled, "I have heard of him. No deal. But I'll take this money anyway."

Darby crushed Clapper's wrist and, as the Captain began to reach for his knife, the writer's grip twisted his arm, sending him to his toes in agony. "You call for help, I'll break both arms before they get me. Now, understand this, Captain, if you take this money, we have a deal."

"All right," Clapper gasped in pain. "All right!"

Darby released his lock. "Are you afraid of the man?"

"I'm no fool, mate," the Captain said angrily, staring at

Darby as though he hadn't seen him until now. "Besides, it makes no sense for me and my crew to risk everything for less money than the oil of one bowhead whale earns."

"How much is that?"

"Plenty. A good-sized bowhead is an awesome beast weighing some sixty-five tons and half as long as my ship. His mouth is so huge he can swallow a whaleboat and six men in a gulp and his blanket of blubber is thicker than your arms. When I finish with him, he'll give us three hundred barrels of oil worth over five thousand."

Darby's moustache bristled. "If you and your men help me capture Wesley Bryant and rescue my friends this morning, I'll gladly pay you the price of ten whales." It would, Darby knew, be a bargain if he could trap Bryant and rescue O'Grady and Lee Ming in addition to retrieving the Central Pacific stocks.

"You've *that* much money?"

"Yes. But we must act at once before he sails, if he hasn't already."

The sea captain's bloodshot eyes met Darby's. "All right, mate. For fifty thousand dollars and this change on the bar, I'd take on Lucifer himself."

Once again the big sea captain grabbed the money and shouted for everyone in the room to hear. "Drink up, you sea rats! It's a bottle of rum for every one of you now before we go to work!"

"I think," Darby said evenly, "they've already had enough rum. Perhaps. . . ."

Clapper leaned in close and his face was vicious. "Listen to me, mate. I misjudged you once and you got away with twisting my arm. I will not misjudge you again. *And,* if we are to have a deal, you must understand that *I* give the orders. Not you. Am I speaking clearly?"

"Quite," Darby replied. He really had no choice but to agree. He needed this motley bunch even more than they needed him.

"But let's get something straight, Captain. If you and these men blunder things this morning and my friends are killed on your account, I swear I'll feed you and each of your men a bottle of rum—but the pleasure will be all mine."

Clapper's complexion paled. He shook and his knuckles whitened as they choked the handle of his knife. But he took the threat and his bottle of rum and then rounded up his men. He wasted few words.

"There's five hundred dollars each for you if we stop him, men! That's more than you earn in a season of risking your freezing hides every day in an open thirty-foot whaleboat. Any man not in this with Captain Clapper better say so now or hold his peace."

No one spoke.

"Good, boys! Now, check your weapons. Make sure they're ready and follow me."

Each man took a bottle of rum and reloaded his weapon. Then, their Captain called them to a shaky line of attention. "All right, boys, I'll not deceive you. Mister Buckingham has hired us to capture The Man of Two Faces."

Darby saw the shock on their drunken faces. One of the smaller ones started to leave his place but Clapper grabbed him by the collar and belted him hard.

"Now," he said, releasing the swaying man and studying the others, "I know something of this demon we must face—we all do, for that matter. His ship, the *Sea Witch*, awaits in the harbor and, if we move quickly in longboats, maybe we can take him by surprise."

"And if we can't?" a sailor dared.

"Then we lose nothing and return here unharmed."

"Now, wait a minute . . ." Darby said.

"That's the deal," Clapper said. "We'll not be shot out of the water."

"Very well. Let's go," Darby answered shortly.

Outside, a weak sun was trying to fight through a heavy fog. Darby thought they were very lucky, because it might hide them until they reached the *Sea Witch*.

They piled into their boats and Darby eased himself forward, the rocking motion at once making him queasy.

"There!" Clapper said, pointing into a mist revealing nothing. "She lies in that direction. Pull hard, you drunken swine. Pull hard!"

They might have been drunk, but Darby was impressed by their rowing ability. Three longboats, with him and Clapper up front, sped through the water. The fog was so heavy they could barely see ten feet ahead.

Out of the mist, like a voice from another world, they heard a sharp command.

"Loosen sails!"

"That's him!" Darby cried.

"Silence!" Clapper roared.

There was a moment when nothing was heard at all. Then, every man in the longboats froze in terror as Bryant screamed, "Man the cannons!"

"Oh, Jeesus!" Clapper breathed.

The fog parted and, as they stared up at the sleek-sided *Sea Witch*, the cannons began to revolve downward.

"Fire when ready!"

Darby saw Bryant through the mist and the man saw him. Then, the man tipped his hat in farewell, his face turned slightly to the north so only part of his eye patch was visible.

A cannon belched a sheet of flame and the ball scorched past Darby's head to bury itself in the bay twenty yards behind them. Darby heard cries and saw the second longboat bounce up on the water's surface, then throw its sailors into the cold, grey waters.

Clapper and his men began to fire but, as the cannons opened up on them from a hundred yards away, Darby saw the terror in their eyes and the desperate futility.

"Jump!"

Then, as a cannonball flamed its deadly path toward them, Darby Buckingham hurled himself into the bay.

The water was paralyzing! He was numb and still going down when their boat took the shot and disintegrated. The cannonball passed not ten feet from his body and, underwater, the shock of it jerked his body into a knot.

Darby held his breath as long as he dared; then, feeling

the coldness seeping through his muscles into his very bones, he came up for air.

Floating wood and crying sailors were everywhere on the bay's calm surface. No one was drunk now.

"Damn you!" the writer cursed at his mortal enemy. "I swear I'll track you down if it has to be to the very ends of this earth!"

Perhaps Bryant spotted him in the tangle of debris, because the man laughed and the sound of it was sick with evil triumph.

"Overhaul the rigging and set course!"

As Darby paddled furiously towards a piece of splintered wood, he saw the *Sea Witch*'s sails fill and the ship began to move quickly away.

Bryant had O'Grady and Lee Ming, *and* the stocks, and now he was after nothing less than that great frozen land they called Alaska.

And, if things continued as they had thus far, he would win his prize. Darby Buckingham knew he was the only one on this earth determined enough to try to prevent that from happening. But so far, he'd lost every encounter to The Man of Two Faces.

It boded ill.

Chapter 9

Captain Clapper was sober now and so was his shivering and bedraggled crew. He was pacing back and forth on the deck of his ship, the *Orion*. It stank of whale blood and blubber, but Darby wasn't aware of those things as he focused on the agitated sea captain.

Clapper stopped pacing and swung about to glare at the writer. "You're daft, mate!"

Darby shivered in his borrowed sailor's clothing. Three sizes too small, the sweater and trousers were tight as a drum, but at least *they* were dry.

"I'm serious. Fifty thousand dollars if you'll pull the anchor and sail for Alaska while the tide is running."

"I'll never catch that foul ship. Nothing afloat could match her speed. And you saw her cannon. My vessel is just a whaling ship! Even if . . ."

"I'll double my offer."

"A hundred thousand dollars!"

"Yes. *If* we stop them before they sabotage the mission of the American envoy to Russia. I know there is time."

"And if there isn't?"

"Then nothing."

"No deal."

"Dammit, Captain! I've told you why I must get to Sitka. If you don't take me, there'll be innocent men slaughtered! The entire territory of Alaska could be at stake."

Captain Clapper's heart was in his treasure chest. "Listen, mate, if I don't hunt the bowhead on our way north, I gamble everything. You say you have a hundred thousand dollars, but there is no way you can get it before we sail. I'm not calling you a liar but neither am I willing to sail after that murdering devil on faith alone!"

"I can get some money," Darby said. He was almost pleading now. "Enough to cover your expenses."

"I'll accept, on one condition."

"Name it."

"If we spot bowhead whale, you agree to let us take them. There'd be precious little time lost."

Darby shook his head. "I'll try someone else."

"None will accept. Not to track the *Sea Witch* after what she did to us."

"I don't even approve of slaughtering whales."

"Damn you, Buckingham! This is no time to question that! And if we don't, the Russians or someone else will. Now, the tide will not last all morning. Do we or do we not have an agreement?"

He was beaten. "All right, blast it!"

"Good." Clapper grinned hugely. "Now there's the matter of that expense money. I will have a sailor row you ashore for it."

"But I'd have to wait for the bank to open!" Darby glanced at the Captain's clock. "That's three hours from now!"

"Yes. In that time, I believe I can just about take on enough fresh water, rum and provisions to get up to Sitka."

"Blast! Can we still make the tide?"

"That's my worry. If you push it, yes. This vessel may not look like much, but she's a stoutly built, bluff-bowed square-rigger planked with New England yellow pine—the best that can be found."

"Yes, but can she run with the wind? It does me no good to arrive in Sitka after Bryant has taken Alaska with his villainous plan."

"Mate, no one knows the northern current and winds as I do. Few can steer a better course. This vessel may not carry the sail of a clipper ship, but she's sheathed with copper over Australian greenheart, a wood that will take the force of an iceberg.''

"Yes, but what. . . ."

"The *Sea Witch* runs lean and trim. In good weather, she'll double our speed. But at night, up in the Alaskan waters where the ice slides into the sea, only a fool would run with the wind. That's where we'll catch him, mate, where the ice mountains float deep and silent.''

Darby understood now. And, as he gazed into the red-veined eyes of Clapper, he got the impression that, maybe, if they didn't sight too many bowhead whales, maybe they would be able to reach Sitka in time.

"All right,'' he said, "we've an agreement. I'll go now and return with the money."

"Sixty-four hundred, Mister Buckingham. That's what it will take to cover this vessel and crew.''

"Very well.''

Clapper grinned. "And if you want to keep rum in their bellies when freezing winds scream off the rivers of ice, then make it an even seven thousand.''

Darby nodded, his mind already leaping to the days which lay ahead. In a few hours, the north chase would begin.

Darby Buckingham anxiously paced the slick wooden deck of the ship *Orion*. How long, he wondered, would this infernal journey take? It seemed like months since he had left San Francisco in pursuit of Wesley Bryant, months of sailing up this devilishly rugged coast with its fog shrouded shores, heavy forests and wild seas crashing against the rocks.

But they were almost there now. They'd sailed through Canadian waters and passed the first heavily forested islands of the Alaskan peninsula. Ahead lay Baranov Island and the Russian fortress of Sitka. Though Clapper was reluctant to give specific days or hours, Darby could tell from the crew that they were very close.

He was more than glad to see this miserable voyage

come to its end. For, while he admired the tough crewmen who labored constantly under the foulest of conditions, he did not like them. The feeling was obviously mutual, for he was the outsider . . . a man viewed only in terms of the money he might pay them if this north chase proved successful. That was why, in the long, rough weeks that had followed their departure, he had lived alone. In his cabin, he had eaten his meals with small enjoyment and examined endlessly the many obstacles which lay ahead. Over and over, he tried to visualize exactly what Bryant would do in his insane attempt to win control over Alaska. The man was a ruthless genius and quite unpredictable. He would strike when least expected and his act would be both decisive and murderous. Darby, however, knew *he* was the one who had the greatest element of surprise if he could arrive in time. That was why, as the days stretched into weeks, Darby Buckingham had agonized over the slowness of the trip.

More and more, they began to see glaciers along the coast and there were times when the great bodies of ice would crack and tons of it would plummet into the ocean, causing tidal waves that Clapper said could be felt hundreds of miles out to sea. And, sometimes, especially at night, the *Orion* would strike smaller ice floes and shake from stem to stern. When that happened, Darby's heart would catch in his throat and he'd brace himself for the chilling cry that the *Orion's* flanks had been pierced. Such things were not uncommon in these arctic waters at this time of year and, even if the crew had time to abandon ship, they often died of exposure at sea or on the rugged coasts.

But the copper sheeting and Captain Clapper's vaunted Australian greenheart proved equal to the blows as they sailed on. And, just as Darby was about to thank his own good fortune that they hadn't faced the delay of sighting and killing the bowhead whales, they did indeed spot one on a cold, windy morning when the sea was running high.

"Whale on the starboard bow!" a voice cried from above decks.

Darby was in his cabin, working on his notes. He leapt to his feet, grabbed his coat and raced up the stairs and out onto the decks above. He followed the pointing finger of Captain Clapper and there, not a mile distant, he saw the monstrous humped back of a whale as it undulated through the ocean, swimming south with a kind of majestic indifference to the human intruders.

"It's a big one, Captain!"

Clapper yanked out a spyglass and peered intently at the whale. "Yes," he said softly, "and it's about time. I was beginning to wonder if we'd ever sight a bowhead on this accursed voyage. So far, I have not made us a penny of profit."

"I've given you expense money," Darby said angrily, "five thousand dollars worth."

"A pittance, mate! *There* is the kind of money I know. And it's waiting for us. Call all hands on deck!"

"Yes, sir!"

Darby stared out through the foggy mist and watched the enormous mammal approach. It was still a mile out but coming in a line that would pass much closer. "Can't we let it go?"

Clapper telescoped his glass and jammed it into his oilskin coat. "Hell no, we can't!" he snapped. "We have an agreement. Besides, we are whaling men. The chase and the kill are in our blood!"

Darby bit back the words he felt inside. They did have an agreement and now, though it aggravated him, he would not renege on his word. Clapper would be allowed to hunt his whale. But, blast! How he detested this delay and the slaughter of such a creature. His eyes swept out to the whale and he felt a shiver of awe at his immensity.

"Man the longboats!" Clapper shouted, as men sprang into action. "Heave to, mates, or I'll have you chase her back to Canada!"

"Buckingham! I'm shorthanded. You'll have to go with them in the lead boat." Clapper grinned. "Besides, I've seen you eyeing our rack of harpoons. It strikes me that I shall have you make the first cast. It should give you something to write in your books."

"Never."

Clapper reached into his oilskin and, this time, instead of a spyglass, he produced a gun. "Mr. Buckingham," he said softly. "I am not asking you to go. I'm ordering you."

Darby stared at the weapon. All around him, men were racing for the boats, other men lowering them over the sides. He saw the big, razor-sharp harpoons. They were vicious-looking weapons with wooden handles five feet long in which a spike nearly half as long was embedded. A barbed hook, curving away from the tip, kept the harpoon from tearing free once it penetrated the whale's hide and coat of blubber.

"Why me?" he grated.

"Because it amuses my fancy. Also, because you have that great power in your arm. I fully expect you to bury the steel all the way to the haft." He pointed at the whale. "Listen carefully, mate, or you will not live to write the story of your adventure. You *must* bury the steel there, just above the fins over the shoulder blade."

"And if I miss?"

"The whale will strike at you with its fluke and God help you if the steersman has not maneuvered the boat from that great tail. The whale will dive and, later, when it surfaces, you will have one more chance."

Darby looked from the gun to the man's eyes. There really was no choice in this matter. He turned and followed the first mate over the side. Down the ropes he scrambled into the longboat where the rough seas had already broached the sides and left its bottom awash.

He sat down fast and they pushed off and began to row up a swell.

"Here," the surly first mate yelled, shoving a harpoon at him. "Good hunting, mate!" Clapper yelled as the other three boats followed.

"Damn him!" the first mate swore. "This is insane. If you miss, we will all be lost to the sea."

"Then *you* do it!"

The man almost took the harpoon. But, at the very last moment, he glanced over his shoulder and saw his Captain watching through the glass. "If I did, he would have me whipped until the hide peeled from my back and ribs. An order disobeyed can mean death."

"Blast you, man! So can a mistake. I do not want to kill the whale."

"Do it. If you value our lives, then do it well. Either way, the whale is already as good as dead. The boats that follow will see to that."

Darby nodded. He understood now and, as their boat rose to crest yet another rolling wave, he clenched the harpoon and saw that they were almost upon the creature. Its skin was the color of grey moss and he could see crusted barnacles. Up close, it was nothing less than awesome. But there was something about the whale that touched him even more forcefully than its size as they approached almost to killing distance. It was the way the huge mammal ignored them as it swam calmly and gracefully south. Darby had the feeling that the creature considered itself invulnerable to the puny threat which approached. This, the writer knew, was the fatal characteristic of the whale and the reason why man, in his flimsy longboats, with a barbaric tool such as the one he now held aloft, was able to destroy the whale instead of being himself destroyed by a single mash of jaws which could strain food from a quarter mile of ocean before swallowing and whose flukes could rupture the strongest hull yet designed.

"Get ready, Buckingham! Remember, strike deep, over and just behind the fins."

"Steersman!" the first mate yelled. "More to port!"

Darby balanced the harpoon. He planted his feet wide apart in the cold sea water which sloshed up around his ankles. They were almost upon the great creature. Its head passed. A flume of mist squirted twenty feet overhead and it was like being rained upon.

"Now!"

Darby drew the weapon back; then, with all his lunging

power, he threw the harpoon. It sailed, trailing rope in its wake, through a twenty-foot distance. He saw the lance pierce the whale's skin and heard a great roar from the ocean, followed by the creature's convulsion. Its tail shot up into the air and crashed down on the surface like the flat of a giant's hand. Water erupted into the skiff. Rope began to spin out from its coil. Every sailor in the boat grabbed ahold and let the line play through their rough, calloused hands as the wounded creature plumed the ocean depths and tried to escape its pain. The boat shot across the water as the whale ran. Big double wakes rooster-tailed up on either side of the bow and Darby Buckingham thought surely they were going to overturn or be swamped.

"Hang on, mates!"

Darby hung on with all his strength. He leaned back against the rope as the wind and the water whipped into his eyes and the boat streamed faster and faster. He wondered desperately what was going to happen if the whale went even deeper. It didn't. And, after what seemed like a lifetime, he felt a gradual slackening of the rope.

"What's he doing?"

"He's sounding, preparing to come up. Be ready. Feel him! Here he comes!"

And he *could* feel the whale rising up from the great depths of the ocean floor. And then, with a thunder of water, the huge 35-ton creature split the ocean's surface and lurched skyward, only to crash back down so violently that the waves were flattened and the longboat was pitched into the air. But, miraculously, it came down with everyone still inside. Then, as he watched, the other boats moved in and cast their harpoons and, as the whale dove again, it was now towing all Captain Clapper's crew as the boats slammed into one another. This time, however, they went only a few hundred yards before the whale tired and, finally, gave up entirely.

"He's done," the first mate said. "He's finished. Good job, mate!"

Darby saw the magnificent creature bob lifelessly on the surface. All the men in the boats were grinning and offered him congratulations but he merely felt ill. They thought he was seasick and laughed at his discomfort. None of them noticed the icy chill in his eyes as he glared back toward the little figure watching them from the deck of the *Orion*.

They towed the whale back to the ship, although it was long, hard work which bent the very oars in their hands. It was almost nightfall when they reached the *Orion* and tied the whale astern. Wearily, the sailors climbed out of the boats and up the latticework rope.

Darby sat alone in the boat trying to compose himself enough to keep from strangling Clapper when and if he managed to get back on deck. He didn't condemn these men for their livelihood, but he did hold Clapper responsible for making him be a part of the act.

"Hey, Buckingham, what's the matter with you down there?" Clapper yelled from the railing above. "I saw you cast steel. Excellent work, mate. Look, the lance is buried to the wood."

Darby looked up. "No more whaling," he snarled furiously. "You've got your damned whale. Now get me to Sitka!"

Clapper's wild eyebrows raised in question. "So it has finally come to this, as I always knew it would. One of us has to give the orders and it shall be *me*."

Darby stood up in the swaying longboat. Something in the tone of the man's voice chilled him.

"Mate," said Clapper, "since you wish to be your own Captain, I give you your wish." He aimed his pistol downward at Darby's face. "Cast off, Mister Buckingham, and row to Sitka, if you can."

"You can't leave me like this. The boat will swamp!"

"With luck, you can get to shore. Sitka lies directly up this coast. Here's a bottle of rum to keep you warm. Goodbye, Captain Buckingham!"

His words caused the entire crew to explode into gales of laughter.

They cast him adrift then, adrift with only the bottle of

rum and a couple of extra harpoons which were kept in reserve.

"We decided to settle for your $7,000," the Captain yelled with delight.

Darby did not answer. There was no reason to. He had been betrayed. And now, as they drifted apart, Darby gazed towards the distant shore, wondering how far it was. Ten miles? Twenty miles?

He stared at the harpoons and the water which sloshed back and forth, growing ever deeper before he slowly laced his thick fingers around the oars. There was no time to waste now. If he had any chance at all for survival, he must row and row hard. His very life depended on it. And, even more importantly, so did the lives of Connor O'Grady, Lee Ming and the American envoy.

With that in mind, he clumsily headed the whaleboat toward the coast, straining his great muscles as hard as ever he had in his life.

Chapter 10

Connor O'Grady's cell was in the forward hold of the *Sea Witch*, up against the bow where the ship took its greatest pounding during heavy weather. The cell itself was remarkably like that of a frontier town jail, except that the floor sloped down in a "V" shape and was constantly moving. During the first days of their northern voyage, Connor had been desperately sick.

Even so, a withered old barnacle of a seaman fed him by pushing a slop tray under the bars with a long mop handle. The man was so cautious that there'd been no possibility of escape. But at least the guard was talkative enough to keep his prisoner informed as to location and sailing conditions. With every day that passed, Connor grew more uneasy. Time was running out quickly and the *Sea Witch* was flying north to Alaska.

On some days, he could feel the ship quiver like a racehorse as her great sails billowed with the wind and they ran fast and strong. On other days, the bad ones, Connor lay in darkness hearing the hull groan under the punishment of the ocean waves. There had been one night when he thought for certain he was going to die as he stood gripping the bars and shouting into the blackness for someone to let him above decks if the ship were going under. It preyed on his mind to think of being drowned deep in the belly of the ship without ever again seeing the sun or the stars. It took all of his self-control during rough weather not to think about the ship plunging down into a giant trough of water, never to rise again.

Connor often wondered why he was being kept alive. Maybe there was no reason. Bryant was a madman. Perhaps he'd completely forgotten him. The possibility grew in Connor's mind, and somehow that seemed the most chilling of all. He thought about Lee Ming and wondered what had become of her. Was she yet alive? He cursed in silent despair upon remembering that Bryant had stated that the punishment for her betrayal was death.

Yet, somehow, Connor believed the girl *was* alive and very near. It was almost as if, in his darkest hours, he could feel Lee Ming's presence and that made him vow to live and free her from Bryant. To do that he now believed he would gladly give his life.

Connor was less certain as to the existence of Darby Buckingham. He remembered hearing cannons roar in San Francisco Bay. It seemed probable that those big guns had been directed at a futile rescue attempt by the Derby Man. Since the attempt had failed, there was little hope that Buckingham had survived. That was another reason Connor swore he would make it through this voyage and exact revenge from Bryant. And so, when the sea grew terrible and he pressed his back against the ship's hull as though somehow he might give it support, he asked only to live long enough that he might repay the ship's captain.

Then, one night, as he lay pondering their fates upon reaching Sitka, three burly sailors came for him. They were armed and he didn't try to resist when they shoved him out of the cell. If he was going to be executed, or thrown into the ocean, Connor figured he would go out fighting, but at least he would die in the sunlight rather than be shot like a rat in the gloom.

His heart was pounding hard when they bound his wrists in front of his body and shoved him towards the stairs. It wasn't easy mounting them, but he did, and when his head popped above the main deck, the sharp, clean air was like a tonic to his numbed senses. He squinted painfully and, though it was not a sunny day, his eyes burned in the unaccustomed light.

"Mind your manners, O'Grady," one of them growled. "You're going to the captain and we've orders to shoot if you run."

He said nothing, but hope stirred inside because it seemed that, if he'd merely been forgotten until now, Bryant would have ordered him killed and be done with it rather than seeing him personally.

"What does your captain want?"

There was no answer, just a sharp prodding as he was shoved forward. One of his guards hammered the door.

"Enter!"

Connor straightened. He was weak from the lack of food and exercise; the climb up the steps had left his legs feeling shaky. He knew he looked terrible. He was unwashed and unkempt—definitely in no condition to fight.

They pushed him inside and Connor sagged against the door for support. His bound hands clenched together and his voice sounded foreign, rusty from disuse. "Good day, Lee Ming, Bryant," Connor said, blinking at the girl and feeling an overwhelming sense of relief that she was alive.

Lee Ming's small hands were clenched at her sides. But that was the only betraying sign of the tension running in her as she bowed. Her eyes looked deep into his own and Connor felt he could read fear and anguish.

"Sit down in that chair, Mister O'Grady," Bryant said, his glance leaping between them. "Lee Ming, why don't you pour our guest some brandy. He appears to be in shock."

Connor's attention snapped back to his mortal enemy. "What do you want from me?"

"I have a proposition. The same one, in fact, that I made to Mister Buckingham that night when Lee Ming betrayed me in San Francisco."

"I think," Connor said with deliberate disdain, "that my answer will be the same as Darby's."

Bryant shrugged. "That would be most unfortunate for you—and her. A tragedy, really."

"What has she to do with it?"

102

"Lee Ming tells me you are a journalist like the *late* Mr. Buckingham."

Connor came out of his seat.

"Sit down," Bryant said with as much emotion as if he were ordering a meal, "or you'll both be dead before this minute has passed."

Connor felt the men against the door. Though he could not see them, he sensed they wanted to come inside. He sat.

"O'Grady, I'm going to skip the formalities and get right to business. Do you or do you not have influence with the editors of the *Boston Globe*?"

"I do. But. . . ."

"Good. You just might have robbed your executioner. My proposition is simple. After I have disposed of the Americans in charge of initiating bargaining for the sale of Alaska, in such a way that it appears to be Russian treachery, I want you to write a full account for the *Boston Globe*. I will, of course, edit it carefully."

"Of course." Connor understood everything now.

"You will then return to San Francisco and telegraph your 'scoop' directly to Boston. When they print the account, other papers will rush to contact you for more details."

"Which I will, piece by piece, let them pry from my lying lips," Connor said dutifully.

"Exactly. I'm certain that the American public—as always—will jump to the most exciting conclusions and make it absolutely impossible for that damned Secretary of State Seward to talk Congress into the purchase."

"This is the price for my staying alive?"

"And Lee Ming," Bryant added. "Please don't bore me with theatrics. Is your answer yes or not?"

"Yes."

"Good." Bryant made a steeple of his fingers. "Of course, I realize you are—at this very moment—wracking your brain in an attempt to trick me. Let me say now that, while you are in San Francisco doing my missionary work,

I will have Lee Ming. When you succeed and *my* offer to buy Alaska is accepted instead of the American's, she is yours.''

"I don't have to ask what you'll do to her if the outcome isn't in your favor."

"Why upset the lady?" Bryant asked quietly.

Connor felt his stomach tighten. His mind and instincts told him there was no use trying to detect a flaw in this plan, for there was none. Perhaps later, when he had had food and a chance to breathe fresh air, he could come up with something—but he doubted it.

As if divining his thoughts, Bryant said, "There is no way you can deceive me. You will soon realize this, even if you don't now. In the meantime, consider what a story like this will do for your *own* career. Overnight, your status will go from nothing to that of a highly respected young journalist. You will be sought by every paper in the country."

Connor grinned sardonically. "Naturally. And once I've accepted some lofty position, I wouldn't dare admit I lied. Very neat, Mister Bryant."

"Thank you. Of course you wouldn't. You'd have a name, a reputation *and* Lee Ming. No man could give up those things. Were I not destined for greatness, I would almost envy your good fortune, O'Grady. As others most surely will."

"Darby told me you were a demon," Connor said aloud, "a diabolical genius. Now, I truly believe him."

"He said that?" Bryant asked with quick interest.

"Yes."

"Well now! That does please me. I never quite got around to telling your late friend this, but apparently the admiration extended both ways. I know this means nothing to you, but I was almost reluctant to have him blown out of the Bay."

He took a glass from Lee Ming and Connor did the same, not daring to look at her closely as the man continued.

"I considered Darby Buckingham my most worthy adversary. The *only* man whom I considered my intellectual complement. His vulnerability and eventual downfall were directly the result of the fact that he operated within the bounds of morality."

Bryant's eye roved about the room as he spoke. "Ill defined as those boundaries may be, they did, nevertheless, limit his options to counter my moves and thus made him fatally predictable. Since destroying him, I have often indulged my intellectual curiosity by wondering—had he also been a man without conscience or ethics—which of us would be sailing to win Alaska."

"How interesting," Connor said cryptically.

"Yes, well, that is done now. We arrive in Sitka in two days. I am unsure if we precede the American ship. In any event, once we drop anchor at Baranov Island, events will move quickly." He began to study a nautical chart on his desk. "Yes, two more days, if the weather holds."

Connor glanced at Lee Ming and wondered if there was any way on earth he might avoid breaking this contract with the devil. It was like selling his soul. Yet, a way had to be found, because Congress would be incensed by the murder of its envoy, angry enough to sell to Bryant without learning the true facts.

He swallowed and tore his eyes away from Lee Ming. He couldn't let Bryant become the Emperor of Alaska! Connor thought of Darby Buckingham and how he'd have found a way to stop this from happening.

The memory of the famous dime novelist made the young Irishman stand taller; no matter what price had to be paid, he would pay it to avenge Buckingham.

Bryant folded his map and hoisted his glass. "To our respective futures, O'Grady—now that you have one."

Connor drank, and he glared right into the single eye of Wesley Bryant. It was like gazing into a black, bottomless hole.

"They've already arrived," Bryant said, gazing intently through his spyglass. "The Americans are anchored in the bay."

105

Connor O'Grady stared into the distance and saw the American ship and, just beyond, the Russian town.

"Will this change anything?"

"Not at all," Bryant grinned. "In a way, it's better. Less delay."

"When?"

Bryant grinned in that twisted way of his. "When will I dispose of the American diplomats?"

"Yes."

"Tonight, of course."

"Tonight?" Connor tried to smile. "I mean, won't you need time to prepare?"

"I'm *always* prepared," the man said with a touch of injury, as though he'd been insulted. "We will be invited by my Russian friends to a banquet at which the Americans will also be present. Drinking. Dancing. You know, the usual children's games. That's when they will be most vulnerable. Tomorrow I'll send you off to San Francisco. Have your story ready for my approval by 10 A.M."

"Sure," Connor muttered, feeling his spirits plummet and wondering how he could possibly hope to change the course of history as it was about to be manipulated.

He realized that Bryant was informing him about the Russian settlement. The town rested under the magnificent snow laden shoulders of Mount Varstovia and faced an archipelago of tiny islands. Connor O'Grady thought the setting extremely beautiful.

"A little background might interest you," Bryant was saying. "Sitka was founded by Alexander Baranov, the man for whom the entire island was named. Baranov was given the title of Governor of Alaska and told by the Russians to build a settlement in the Americas to reap the wealth of the fur trade. He carried out these orders with courage and resourcefulness. Baranov died an honored man for his work here. Unfortunately, he died on the trip home to receive his long overdue reward."

"What is that huge spire-topped building?" Conner asked.

"Saint Michael's Cathedral," Bryant said with little interest. "See how the village is fortified? Three years after Baranov founded the town, it was suddenly attacked by a tribe called the Tlingits while he and most of his riflemen were away hunting. They killed and beheaded hundreds of citizens and carried off most of the women and children."

"What did Baranov do about that?"

"He fortified the settlement and attacked the Indians in turn, but they gave him a rough battle—one that eventually became a siege. Finally, by bombarding their village from ships and attacking on land, they drove the Tlingits away. Now they are quite domesticated and hunt both whale and sea otter for the Russians in these waters. But, all up and down this and other islands, there are small bands of renegade Tlingits who kill any white man they can. Pity anyone shipwrecked on this coast."

He pointed to a low hill by the water. "See the mansion there?"

"Yes," Connor said, filing away the information about the hostile Indians.

"It's still called Baranov's Castle. That's where we'll meet the present Russian governor and where—if we allowed it—the negotiations for the sale of Alaska would take place."

Connor studied the two-storied castle with its swirling Russian flag beating the wind. So, he thought, that must be where the attack will take place. "It's impressive."

"Baranov himself is one of my few heroes. If he hadn't been shackled by the Russian nobility and given almost no help in his colonization work, he'd have taken all of California."

"Didn't they establish a fort?"

"Yes, Fort Ross, 65 miles above San Francisco. I think it was in 1812, and they expended so much energy trying to protect themselves from attack that they failed in their primary mission, which was to provide their hungry mother colony here at Sitka with wheat, barley, vegetables and beef. Because of that, and also because the local Indians they'd enslaved robbed them so effectively, the colony failed.''

He lit a cigar, his face reflecting the irony. "Baranov wasn't at Fort Ross or they'd have succeeded and, today, I might be on the threshold of owning upper California as well as Alaska.''

Connor held his tongue and bit back the angry words he wanted to hurl at this power-crazed zealot.

"As it was," Bryant said with unconcealed contempt, "they practically gave Fort Ross away to John Sutter in 1841 for a pittance of thirty thousand dollars. By such acts of stupidity are empires won and lost.''

"I'll remember that," Connor said quietly.

Bryant looked at him askance. "O'Grady, I don't trust you yet but if you play it straight and smart, you just might have a future in my Alaska. I'll have great powers to bestow on those who are loyal.''

Connor nodded without answer and the man beside him pitched his cigar into the bay. "I must take command now. Soon we will depart for Baranov's Castle to be greeted by my Russian friends. I will have hot water and a new suit of formal clothing delivered to your cabin at once. We can't have you looking like a galley slave, now can we?''

"No," Connor replied hotly as the man chuckled and left him beside the railing.

For long minutes, he brooded and agonized over how he might stop Wesley Bryant before tonight's assassination was done. Then he rubbed his eyes harshly with his knuckles and whispered fervently, "God help me, but I'd give anything if the Derby Man were here now to tell me what to do!''

Chapter 11

Darby eyed the rocky coast with a mixture of relief and fear. The whaleboat was a foot awash in water now and taking on more every minute. Rowing was nearly impossible as the craft wallowed in the heavy sea.

There'd been no choice but to head for shore and try to beach safely. That hadn't been as easy as he'd at first thought, because there were almost no beaches of any kind, only vicious rocks against which the thundering waves smashed into a towering spray. It would not be fun landing in such places. He and the boat would be destroyed.

So, he'd kept rowing until now, finally, he was madly angling the waterlogged whaleboat toward a small, driftwood-strewn cove. The trouble was that in the wind and sleet, he had a bad time trying to judge the distance and now, as the current swept him inward, he was on a direct collision course with a line of kelp-draped rocks. They foamed with white anticipation.

"Row, man!" he grunted, pulling so hard the oars bent near their breaking point and he was nearly leaning at a forty-five-degree angle. "Row!"

The pounding breakers thundered in his ears, and suddenly, he felt the craft being lifted as though by a giant's hand. Up, up, the whaleboat rose until it seemed to hang in the air, then it sped toward shore, going faster than any locomotive, hellbent for destruction. The ocean seemed to pour in all around him in a rushing wall of foam. The oars were ripped from their mountings and torn from Darby's fists. Down he raced, feeling as though the bottom of the sea must have dropped from the world. He closed his eyes, knowing he was going to hit the rocks and die.

A horrendous grinding shock threw him sprawling as the boat's hull tore over a hidden reef and, suddenly, the roar was gone and he washed smoothly up onto the sandy beach.

Darby blinked in amazement. For the first time in weeks, the surface upon which he sat did not rock. He'd made it. Perhaps, he thought, staring down at the harpoons, the bottle of rum and his blister-covered hands, perhaps he was destined to stop Bryant. There could, he reflected solemnly, be no other reason for his miraculous delivery from the jaws of death. But then, he reasoned, maybe he was grasping at straws. He would still have to go back out onto the ocean and he had no idea how to get back past the reef and breakers, much less. . . .

These worries vanished as, on the perimeter of the beach, a group of Indian warriors, dressed in heavy seal-skins and carrying ivory-bladed lances, moved forward for the kill.

Darby glanced frantically back at the angry ocean. There wasn't one chance in a million that he had either the time or the talent necessary to escape that way. He took a deep breath and grabbed a harpoon in each fist, then jumped out of the swamped boat.

"Friend!" he called, gazing hopefully from one to the next. "Drop the weapons. We talk!"

They didn't even blink. Stupid try anyway, he thought miserably, staring at them as they edged closer.

Suddenly, the biggest warrior sprang forward, screaming like a wild man and cocking his lance back to throw.

Darby crouched in his fighter's stance and, when the lance came whistling through the air, he ducked. The weapon sailed by and he heard it strike water. That's when he reared back and, with all his strength, let his first harpoon fly. Despite its great size and weight, the harpoon shot across the beach and kept flying until it struck a pine tree and buried its steel almost to the haft. The attacker tripped on a tangled piece of driftwood and fell.

Darby flipped the other harpoon from his left to his right hand and waited for the attacker to charge again. He wasn't going to spear him on the ground, but neither did he intend to let the Indian skewer him.

The Tlingits had momentarily forgotten Darby. They were gaping at the quivering harpoon which now was embedded in the tree to an astonishing depth.

One of them pivoted and hollered to the Indian who'd tripped while attacking. It must not have been a compliment, for the big man's flat face convulsed with anger and he jumped to his feet, drawing out a knife. Only twenty feet of beach was between them and the Indian came in faster now that the sand was damp and more firm.

Darby feigned a throw and the Indian dove to the ground. The writer smiled grimly at the clumsy attempts at deception and discovered that an Alaskan Indian is capable of flushing with embarrassment. Wounded in pride, the man once again jumped up and this time Darby knew nothing but force would stop him.

So, as the Tlingit lunged, Darby parried his thrust, then swung the long wooden handle and knocked him senseless.

"Come on!" he yelled, gesturing them forward. "Let's be done with this."

His roar of anger caused a storm of controversy among them. Darby lowered his harpoon and anxiously awaited their next move. He knelt and checked to see if the Indian stretched at his feet was still alive. He was. One thing for certain, the fella was going to look like an aspiring unicorn with that knot on his forehead.

The argument apparently focused on the harpoon buried in the tree. They'd forgotten about him for the moment, knowing full well he wasn't going anywhere. One after another of them gripped the harpoon and tried to pull it loose. They even hopped up and planted their hairy boots on the tree's trunk to give themselves more leverage as they strained and grunted in futility.

The harpoon was obviously in to stay. Its barb was

111

designed to keep it from tearing loose and, wood or whale's blubber, the result was the same.

"If you need it that bad, then ask!" he shouted at them as he tromped forward. They stared with suspicion but parted in definite awe at his great size. Darby grabbed the wooden handle and pulled.

Nothing happened.

The Indians surveyed each other. Several gestured at him with new boldness and sudden contempt. It didn't take a genius to decide the only hope he had in the world was in freeing this damned harpoon.

The writer planted his feet against the tree as they'd done and, as always when beginning the greatest of his powerful feats of strength, his neck appeared to sink into massive shoulders as his arms began to cord with muscle.

"Come on!" he rasped as his breath exploded from his gritted teeth in short bursts. Darby's entire 235 pounds became a pulling machine and, though it was cold and raw, beads of sweat sprang from his pores as his great muscles shivered with exertion.

"Come on, you! . . ."

The shaft ripped loose and Darby recoiled from the tree as if he'd been triggered by a powerful spring. He crashed on the beach with the harpoon clutched to his chest, point up to the sky, then he sat up, ready to die. But the murderous Tlingits began laughing.

Laughter, it turned out, *was* good medicine. Either that or Darby figured they must have been mightily impressed by his harpoon-throwing and retracting ability. Even the big Indian that he'd clobbered with the harpoon didn't seem to bear any lasting grudges.

They took the writer to their village and Darby was struck by the clean organization of things. The Indians lived in well-built wooden houses, each with a seaworthy vessel much like the whaling boat he'd arrived in placed beside their doors. He did see what he thought were slaves working on hides and tending fires, and Darby reminded himself that this was not a harmless tribe; had they not found his strength so impressive, he'd have been dead hours ago.

Intricately carved totem poles surrounded their village and Darby viewed them closely. He decided they were constructed for the benefit of a host of animal and bird gods. Most were stained, probably by boiling various plants and roots. If he hadn't been so eager to get to Sitka, he'd have tried to draw some pictures or at least have taken copious notes of his findings. He wasn't certain, but from what he observed, this tribe did not trade with the Russians. The few Russian shirts and coats he did see were ripped and stained with old dried blood. It was enough to make a white man jittery.

They wanted his knife, bottle of rum, cigars and the harpoons. In exchange for their agreement to take him near Sitka, they would let him keep one harpoon and the white man's boat. Though they couldn't speak his tongue, it was pretty clear to the Derby Man that they thought the whaleboat was a sloppy piece of work.

He agreed to their terms because, when he tried to hide one of his cigars, they suddenly became very excitable, and not with pleasure. He gave the Cuban cigar back in a hurry.

That night, the Tlingits smoked and drank some kind of vile brew that made them extremely boisterous. For hours on end, they howled at each other and up at the stoic totem poles. They did not become quiet until dawn, when they fell into a twitching sleep. When they woke Darby up several hours later, he was not a happy man. His eyes burned, his head throbbed and even the little brew he'd been forced to drink left his mouth tasting as if he'd chewed raw grasshoppers.

Even so, as they all piled into the boats, the sea was calmer; Darby pulled his collar up around his neck and counted himself a very, very lucky man. They'd managed to indicate that the hated Russian settlement was only one day's journey.

Darby nodded as the ocean spray stung his bloodshot eyes. What I wouldn't give, he thought bleakly, for one halfway decent cigar and a pot of coffee.

He closed his eyes and tried not to shiver or to think of his own discomfort and how they'd taken his clothes and made him wear a stinking collection of animal skins. Blast! Couldn't they at least have scraped off all the lard!

"To hell with it," he rumbled darkly. If he could just reach Sitka before O'Grady, Lee Ming and the Americans were eliminated, he'd not complain.

In a desperate attempt to rationalize his sad state of appearance, he told himself that the smelly skins would perhaps conceal his true identity from Bryant until he was able to wrap his fingers around that devil's throat. He tried very hard not to think of what he'd do if Bryant had already carried out his terrible plan and left Sitka.

Instead, Darby just huddled in the animal skins and wondered how he'd ever gotten into this whole mess. By all that was just and fair, he should be with Dolly Beavers now, perhaps dining in some fine San Francisco restaurant, sipping good Bolivian coffee and puffing on a Cuban cigar.

Blast!

That evening, Bryant, Lee Ming and Connor O'Grady were rowed ashore to attend a grand feast at Baranov's Castle.

"I am armed, Mister O'Grady, and should you have any delusions of grandeur, rest assured that Lee Ming will be always at my side. The process to eliminate the Americans has already been put into motion and any foolish attempt to save them would result in unnecessary deaths."

Connor swallowed drily. "I understand," he said in a thick voice.

"Good. Then I suggest you practice smiling and at least appear to enjoy yourself tonight. These Russians are people of rank and privilege; many are former naval officers, one a baron, the Governor and his wife are Prince and Princess Maksutov, both of whom would be deeply offended by any sign of your current dejected appearance. Lee Ming?''

"Yes, Master."

"You will tell the Governor and his friends that you are not feeling well and do not wish to dance. Under no circumstances are you to leave my side—the penalty for disobedience is death. The same will hold should you leave our company, O'Grady."

He said nothing. But more than anything in life, Connor wanted to tell her that everything would be fine. Somehow.

A carriage was waiting for them at the pier and they were immediately whisked away to the castle where a dozen armed Russian soldiers stood rigid guard before a great copper-shielded doorway.

A butler took their hats and coats and Connor was amazed at the richness of the mansion's interior. Everywhere he looked, he saw gilded figurines and Russian tapestries hanging from the walls. The alabaster-pillared hallway, into which they moved, was filled with dignified couples, talking loudly and gesturing with their glasses.

Music played and several young couples were already dancing. Connor shook his head. He'd never seen anything to match the elegance of this place; neither had he ever had such a feeling that time was running out. Where were the Americans? How many of them were in attendance?

"This way," Bryant said, shaking a tall officer's hand and then moving on quickly as he spoke greetings to almost everyone they passed.

Connor followed obediently. Most of the conversation was in Russian and therefore unintelligible to him, though Lee Ming and Bryant seemed quite fluent.

"And this," Bryant said, his tone indicating great respect, "is Prince Dimitri Maksutov and his wife, the lovely Princess Maria Maksutov. Bow, please."

Connor and Lee Ming did so as the Russian couple warmly greeted Bryant. When Connor straightened, he saw that the princess was actually quite lovely in her satin dress with a prim bustle. The prince was a balding man, stocky and fortyish. Both of them shook Connor's hand and, in stilted English, the prince asked him if he'd enjoyed the voyage.

"It was . . . an unforgettable experience," Connor replied, noting the instantaneous flare of warning in Bryant's eyes. "I am greatly honored that you and the princess invited me to attend."

They smiled stiff, quick little smiles, and it was the princess who said, "We try to look happy tonight; we are not. You see, it is Czar Alexander who wishes to sell Alaska, though we have begged him to reconsider."

"You like it here?" Connor was surprised. These refined aristocrats just didn't appear the types that would enjoy the hardships of the Alaskan frontier.

"Yes," the princess answered in a sad voice. "My husband is the thirteenth governor since Alexander Baranov. Isn't that called an unlucky number by you Americans?"

Connor could feel the intensity of Bryant's gaze. "Superstition," he mumbled.

"Nevertheless," the prince said, "I have little choice but to begin negotiations. Everyone here knows of our feelings—even the American ambassadors. To hide those feelings from those with whom we must deal would be to lie."

Maksutov gestured toward a pair of gentlemen and Connor studied them intently. "I see."

"If they would just give us more time!" the prince complained bitterly. "Yet, the harvest of furs is poor now and the hunting gets worse each year. Mother Russia cannot sustain the heavy burden my colony puts on her at present."

"It is *no* burden!" Princess Maria cried in protest. "Dimitri, for years this colony has enriched the czar's coffers. It will do so again! They say there is gold. . . ."

"Maria, you know as well as I that these are merely rumors being circulated by the Indians who fear Americans more than ourselves."

"But I have seen this gold!"

116

Prince Maksutov firmly took his wife's arm and patted it as he would the head of a lovable but ignorant dog. "They show her some gold. She believes because of her love for Alaska."

"I understand," Connor replied.

"Thank you. Maria," the prince said with weary patience. "It is time to call our guests for dinner. Tonight, we have pork, octopus, Alaskan crab and iced red salmon. Your favorites, Mister Bryant."

"Ah, yes, especially the way that Lee Ming's brother prepares them. Is he still in your kitchen?" Bryant asked off-handedly.

The prince nodded.

"Good. I took the liberty of having a special case of French wine sent up earlier this afternoon for those of your guests who would enjoy such a treat."

"Excellent. And now, let us try to make ourselves be happy tonight. For who knows what is on the morrow."

Yes, Connor thought, taking Bryant's lead and bowing as the royal couple departed. Who knows?

Only one thing was certain—if he didn't think of something before they returned to the ship, the two American gentlemen would have no tomorrow.

Chapter 12

It was dark when the Tlingits quietly rowed into Sitka's harbor and landed their wooden boats. Darby could sense their apprehension and guessed that these Indians both feared and hated the Russians. So he paid his fare and, because words would be useless to express his gratitude for a safe delivery, he shook each warrior's hand.

These people were not long on sentimentality or farewells, so they pushed off, leaving him with an empty whaleboat and a harpoon for protection. Up in Sitka, he heard music and laughter coming from what appeared to be a palace which overlooked the harbor.

Darby hadn't failed to recognize the hated *Sea Witch,* or the American ship anchored not far away. He'd strongly considered asking the Tlingits to deliver him to the American vessel. Once aboard, he could have sounded the warning. But what, he'd paused to ask himself, if his warning was ignored by some stubborn young officer? With cold objectivity, he had to admit his present appearance did not exactly inspire confidence.

So he'd vetoed the idea. Now, as he surveyed the castle, he decided that he must have arrived in time or there surely wouldn't be a celebration going on—unless Bryant owned the place and was glorying in conquest.

Darby thought this unlikely but resolved to exercise the greatest care in his approach. He was cold, stiff and tired and still a bit queasy from the previous night's experience. Yet he was alive, and that in itself was something of a miracle considering what he'd gone through in only a bit more than twenty-four hours.

He labored up the hillside and then dove into some bushes when he saw the Russian soldier on guard. As he tried to catch his breath and figure out his next move, another soldier emerged from the gloom after having completed a solitary patrol.

Darby retreated back into the darkness, then skirted around the mansion, catching glimpses of refined couples through the windows. That, he decided, meant that he'd arrived in time, for Wesley Bryant did not attract handsome people. His idea of a celebration might closer resemble a pagan orgy or a public whipping.

The back and side entrances were locked. He checked each one and found the doors to be of solid iron and totally impregnable. Darby cursed and prowled out of eyesight back to watch the guards once more.

Perhaps he could simply wait until the affair was over and Bryant emerged. But then what could he do? Harpoon the man? Bryant would be armed and there was no real cover from which to spring. Besides, what if the man intended to carry out his murderous plan this very evening?

The writer dared not risk the possibility. With that in mind, he took a deep breath, then stood up and walked into the lamplight where the Russians could observe him.

One yelled something and they all swung about with their rifles coming to their shoulders. "Friend! American!" Darby bellowed, reaching as if to grab the Big Dipper.

They didn't open fire, though he could see it was a very near thing. Maybe they understood the word "American" and realized he wasn't really a Tlingit Indian. Whatever the reason, they showed no signs of trusting him as they stalked warily forward.

"American," he said again.

One of the soldiers raised a lantern to peer at him closely. His nose twitched with disgust and he repeated, "American?"

"Yes," Darby replied, nodding emphatically.

They went into a conversation, their rifles never leaving

their target. Suddenly, from inside the room, there was a scream followed by shouts.

The Russians swung around and dashed for the entrance. Darby was right on their heels. He skidded to a halt in the massive hallway and, in one quick glance, he understood everything.

Connor O'Grady was on the floor cradling Lee Ming's head in his lap and tears were streaming down his face. The redhead looked up and Darby's eyes followed his gaze to locate Wesley Bryant.

"You poisoned her with the wine!" Connor raged.

"You're insane!" Bryant snarled.

Connor laid the girl's head down on the polished marble floor and stood.

"I'm not insane, Bryant. Lee Ming is dead because she must have realized that your wine was intended only for Americans—that Russians would prefer vodka. That's why she drank it first, because she believed there was no way to stop you from murdering her brother if she warned anyone."

Bryant laughed and his assurance was frighteningly convincing as he smiled at the assemblage of Russians and Americans. "Prince Dimitri, Princess Maria, I must apologize for this man's behavior. He was, I'm now convinced, hopelessly in love with Lee Ming. I . . . I didn't have the heart to tell him she was cursed with a fatal heart condition. Any excitement. . . ."

"That's a lie!" Connor yelled.

The room buzzed with whispers in English and Russian.

"Young man," Bryant said, his voice icy now with warning, "I loved her too, but I won't be accused." He drew back his coat and revealed a gun.

"The hell with you!" Connor shouted. "Give me a weapon."

Darby Buckingham saw the small tick of muscle in Bryant's cheek and heard the man say, "Why, of course, O'Grady, if that is the *only* solution."

Darby stepped in behind one of the Russian soldiers and

tore the man's rifle away, then shoved him sideways as he jumped into the hallway. "Freeze, Bryant!"

The arrogant confidence that had ridden so boldly on the man's scarred face vanished as he gaped in disbelief. "You!" he whispered.

"None other," Darby said with a malicious grin.

"They'll never let you out of here alive, Buckingham. Look!"

Darby glanced around. The soldiers had recovered and, though extremely agitated, looked ready to fire. "Tell these people the truth."

"I have." Bryant whispered something in Russian and the soldiers took aim.

"The wine *is* poisoned!" Connor shouted. "Prince Maksutov, simply ask Mister Bryant to drink from that bottle and none of this bloodshed need occur!"

The Governor of Sitka detached himself from his wife and countrymen.

"Would you, whatever your name is, agree to give up your weapon if the wine is good?" the Russian asked.

Darby took a deep breath. "Connor, are you *certain* it was the true cause of Lee Ming's death? Because, if we are taken prisoner, this game is lost."

"I'm sure." Connor gazed down at the beautiful Chinese girl at his feet. His voice was choking. "She knew it and now so do I."

Darby was satisfied. Lee Ming was dead and he was willing to risk his own neck that she hadn't died of heart failure.

"All right, sir," he replied to the Russian, "if Bryant agrees to drink the wine, I'll hand over the rifle."

Prince Maksutov and the two American diplomats visibly relaxed. They were not dealing with a total madman after all. "Then it is settled. Wesley, please show this . . . man the excellence of your gift."

Bryant swallowed loud enough for everyone to hear. "Your Highness," he said, a conciliatory tone in his voice, "don't you realize that these two fiends are merely stalling for time? They are both insane enough to. . . ."

But the Russian cut him off with an angry swipe of his hand. "No more! Drink the wine, please. I will not have the lives of all my guests endangered! Do as I say."

Bryant knew he was beaten. And, as Darby watched his arch enemy, he almost felt a touch of admiration for the supreme control it must have taken for such a man to accept the loss of an empire. Because that was what had just happened, though only the three of them were aware of the fact.

"Very well. As your friend and loyal servant, I once again comply with your wishes."

"Thank you, Wesley. I am ashamed to ask you to do this, but . . ." he gestured around the hall, ". . . the safety of my guests demands every precaution."

"I understand."

Bryant stepped toward the place at the banquet table where Lee Ming had been seated. As he passed the body of the girl and the distraught young Irishman, he reached over and picked up the wine bottle.

"Bordeaux, an excellent vintage, bottled by master vintners nearly twenty years ago. It will be a pleasure to. . . ."

Even as he was speaking, he swung the bottle by its neck and viciously bashed O'Grady over the left eye as he flipped his revolver from his holster.

"Don't move, Buckingham! Drop the gun or your friend is a dead man!"

Darby cursed himself for not killing Bryant when he could have. Yes, he'd have lost his own life to the soldiers, but *anything* was preferable to this!

"Buckingham!" Bryant screeched, holding the dazed Irishman as a shield. "Drop the rifle or so help me I'll kill your friend!"

Darby hurled the weapon to the marble floor saying, "Give it up. You've lost the game. Alaska will *not* be yours!"

"Your Highness, order your soldiers to throw down their weapons!"

Maksutov was in shock. His face said more plainly than words that he had not fully accepted this surprising turn of events.

"Do it, Dimitri!"

The prince jerked himself into reality. One minute, he was just standing before them with his mouth open, the next he was shouting orders and rifles were clattering onto the polished floor.

"Good. Now, Mister Buckingham, since you are such a big, powerful man, I am going to use you as a shield as you obligingly carry O'Grady out the door and down to the harbor."

As Darby was about to protest, the man hissed, "Do not insult your considerable intelligence by arguing with me. You know my back is to the wall and I'll kill without hesitation."

"Yes," Darby whispered, "I know."

"Dimitri, Maria," Bryant said, "I really am sorry that you had to learn of my intentions in this way. You've been good friends and it was my hope to have visited you often in St. Petersburg. As for the sale of Alaska, since I can see no possibility of having her, I hope you drive a sharp bargain. It ought to be worth at least ten million, though you'll never get it."

"Why," the prince asked in a hushed voice, "did you have to kill Lee Ming?"

Bryant's eye fell to the girl. "She betrayed me in San Francisco and I forgave her. But at last I came to realize she would betray me again—as she did, just moments ago, at your table."

His voice cracked with bitter fury. "Had it not been for her, I would have done it! She is fortunate beyond words to be dead. Let's go, Mister Buckingham. This party is over."

Darby took the sagging body of O'Grady and lifted him as easily as most would a child. He could feel the gun barrel pressed to his spine as they started backing out of the hall.

"Dimitri, you will not, nor will your American friends, pursue me."

He reached out and grabbed the princess and, in one quick motion, held her locked in his free arm.

"No!" Maksutov shouted.

Bryant took the gun from Darby's back and pressed it to the woman's temple. "If *anyone* tries to stop me, she joins Lee Ming. Maria is my protection until we leave your harbor. At the north point of this island I will have her rowed safely to shore."

"Why should I believe that?" Maksutov demanded, his face pale with worry and indecision.

"Because I have absolutely nothing to gain by harming your wife. My only need for her is to prevent you from opening fire with your cannon and destroying my vessel before I leave this harbor."

"Your Highness," Darby said, "I believe him. It would be foolish for the man to incur the wrath of the entire Russian empire. If he injured your wife, he knows your navy would hunt him to the ends of the earth."

The Governor of Alaska glanced from one to the other. "Very well," he said in defeat, then shouted orders in Russian for them to pass.

Connor O'Grady stiffened in Darby's arms and his eyelids fluttered as they backed out of the castle's entrance. There was a fresh wind coming off the ocean and Darby thought about how the *Sea Witch* would probably be unstoppable after it passed beyond range of Sitka's cannon.

They started down the trail toward the water. There was just enough moonlight to see the path clearly. Maria Maksutov's face was as white as a headstone, but she did not whisper or cry out in pain as Bryant roughly led her down to his ship.

O'Grady shifted in his arms and, as they approached the water and the breaking waves grew loud, he whispered, "Darby."

"Shhh!" the dime novelist buzzed. "Are you all right?"

Connor nodded.

"Then be ready!"

"Who goes there?" a voice called up from the shore.

"It's me," Bryant answered sharply. "Get up here. Quick!"

Darby heard the running footsteps and the sound of rocks overturning as the crew of the longboat struggled up from the beach. Once they arrived, he knew his chances of escape were nonexistent.

So he tripped and fell heavily, dropping O'Grady on the slope.

Bryant whirled, his gun coming to rest on Darby. "You're not fooling anyone, Buckingham! For you, this is the end."

He cocked his pistol. The princess cried in alarm and struggled helplessly. Darby crouched in the moonlight, staring at the dark silhouette, and the gun that pointed at him, ready to blow away his life. And, in that last awful moment as he knelt on the stony rubble below Baranov's Castle, he realized that, once again, he'd run out of time and luck.

Connor O'Grady had to throw the rock even though he was lying flat on his back. It wasn't a hard throw, or even an especially accurate one as it slammed into Bryant's knee. But it *did* knock Wesley Bryant's aim off long enough for Connor to roll to his feet and spring at the man just as he fired again.

The bullet that was meant to take Darby's life exploded against Connor's shoulder and then he heard shouting and gunshots as, once more, Darby's powerful arms lifted him. Connor felt jarring pain sweep up to enfold him in blackness as the writer scrambled madly into the night in a dash for safety. Just before Connor yielded to the darkness, he thought he felt Darby falling. He wasn't certain. All he knew as he slipped into unconsciousness was that the rancid furs Darby Buckingham wore stank like hell.

Chapter 13

Darby had no chance of stopping Wesley Bryant. When the man had started shooting, he'd been stretched out headlong, facing downslope. He didn't have a prayer until Connor threw his rock. Now, as his thick legs drove him deeper into the night, he could hear Princess Maksutov crying for help as Bryant and his crew opened fire at his retreating form. Bullets whined about him, but Darby knew he was only a vague shadow which was fading as he stretched out the distance between them.

When the shots died in the night and he heard the unmistakable sound of oars slapping water, Darby stopped running and sagged to his knees. His stubby fingers ripped open O'Grady's shirt and probed the wound. He could feel the warm blood and he bitterly berated himself for letting this happen.

He tore part of Connor's shirt away and stuffed it into the wound, satisfied that neither the lung nor the heart was pierced. Still, it required urgent professional attention. Darby picked up his young friend and hurried up toward the castle. His face was grim and he said aloud in his anger, "Connor, I haven't done too well so far in bringing The Man of Two Faces to justice, but I'm not finished, any more than I was in San Francisco Bay. What he did to Lee Ming and you only makes me more resolute to finish him off. He'll get away this time, but even if I have to hire the entire Russian Navy we'll find him!"

But Connor O'Grady didn't answer. He was mercifully unconscious when Darby gave him over to a Russian doctor and choked, "Prince Maksutov, if your physician vows to take good care of my friend, I'll promise to catch Bryant and return your wife."

"Mister O'Grady will be given the best of medical care," Maksutov said. "As for your promise, it is not necessary. I'll go after them. Do you wish to sail with me?" he asked quietly, his eyes scanning the hills bordering the harbor.

Darby knew what the man was thinking. If it wasn't for his wife being held captive, he would unleash the cannon. The sails of the *Sea Witch* were even now expanding like the opening of a white rose against the backdrop of black water.

"I'll come," Darby said, watching the doctor order Connor to be taken to his offices. "You would be hard pressed to stop me, sir."

The man looked at Darby now. "Tell me," he whispered, "what you said in there when he took Maria, was it true? Had I not believed you, I would have ordered my soldiers to stop him at any cost."

"It *was* true," Darby replied. Then, to himself, he added, I hope.

It *was* true. They found Princess Maria stranded on a lonely point of rock, exactly where Bryant had said she would be. The woman was shivering in the cold and more angry than scared, now that she'd had time to reflect on her ill treatment.

"It is over," the Russian said. "Maria, I will take you home."

Darby steeled himself to object. "It is *not* over. Not as long as that man is free."

The Russian's face darkened. "My wife needs medical attention. Your friend made it necessary that our doctor remain in Sitka; now, we must return at once for Maria's sake."

"But. . . ."

"Do not argue with me, Mister Buckingham."

Darby gripped the railing. "Then, I'll require the use of a longboat! I will *not* let him escape. Not after what he's done."

"You are crazy," the Russian said, eyeing him closely. "In these waters or ashore among the Tlingits, you wouldn't survive a week. Reconsider. Perhaps you can convince your American countrymen to join the hunt."

"Dimitri," the princess interrupted, her voice hard and flat with resolve, "I am safe, but outraged by my treatment. Do not let this man adrift to perish. Would it be so wrong to help him avenge the one who deceived us?"

"No," the prince said, quite obviously surprised at her intervention, "but my duties, the negotiations. Later. . . ."

"It may be too late then," Darby argued. "Prince Maksutov, are you certain that Bryant will not attempt to regain Sitka—by force next time, before the sale is completed?"

The prince didn't look certain of anything. "My orders are to enter into negotiations," he began stubbornly, "not to chase a madman up and down this maze of coastal islands."

"Three days," Darby pleaded.

"And what do you hope to find? Surely, you must realize that the *Sea Witch* is faster than this vessel."

"Yes, but accidents can happen." Darby frowned; even to himself his logic sounded faulty and desperate though he pushed on with it. "Perhaps Bryant will get careless. Perhaps we'll run across another ship. What I must know is if the *Sea Witch* is bound for China or intends to remain in these waters. I would think you would share my desire."

"Dimitri, this man predicted I would be released unharmed and, in doing so, may have saved my life. Grant his request."

Together, they were too much for the man to overrule. "Very well," he said gruffly. "Three days ought to give us enough time to chart his course. I have many friends in these waters as well as our Indian hunters. He cannot escape their eyes."

"Which way did he sail after leaving you?" Darby asked, feeling hope surge through his veins.

She revolved and pointed.

"Are you certain?" the prince asked in a tone which indicated disbelief.

"Of course," she replied firmly. "What else did I have to do on those awful rocks while waiting? They sailed east."

Darby stared in the direction of Canada. His view was obscured by yet another of the endless chain of islands. To him, they all looked identical to Baranov's Island—heavily forested and incredibly rugged. Probably loaded with Tlingit Indian villages.

"Why would he sail that way?" Darby asked aloud.

"Perhaps to confuse us. He is, as you know, Mister Buckingham, rather brilliant. These islands could be used to play games of . . . how do your children say it?"

"I believe," Darby answered, "it's hide-and-seek."

"Yes, that is the one. He may also be merely skirting to the other side of Baranov's Island to dash south before rounding the lower tip to sail for China. There is one other great danger."

"What's that?"

The prince's eyes hardened. "That he might wish us to follow and set his trap. Should he sink us, he might even be able to plunder and pillage Sitka itself."

Darby turned the frightening idea over in his head. Bryant was insane enough to do any of those things; yet, for some reason that he didn't quite understand, the writer rejected the possibility. Bryant would seek escape. And why not? He had the Central Pacific stock aboard ship and, therefore, enough funds to buy the territory to satisfy his craving for becoming a ruler.

Darby shook his head. "What if he turns north? Sails up the inland passage?"

"He could eventually pass around Chichagof Island into the Gulf of Alaska, or he could go up the channel another 160 kilometers until he comes to the small Indian village at his head called Skagway. I am told it is near a mountain

129

pass leading into what the Canadian people call the Yukon. A terrible place.''

"I've heard of it, a snowy hell where only the Eskimos can survive."

"Not quite true," Maksutov said. "Canadians and Americans are finding gold there even now, but it is a hard land. I do not think he would go there."

Darby said nothing. But the more he mulled it over, the more he began to think that the Yukon, with all its unsettled land and vast riches, was *exactly* the kind of place to which Bryant would be attracted, for the very same reasons he'd desired to possess Alaska.

It was actually the fourth day, but even Prince Maksutov wasn't counting now because his informants had, indeed, directed them into the long northward channel at the head of which lay the village of Skagway. If this was true, they had the *Sea Witch*. There was no escape.

Everyone grew tense as they sailed on, perhaps into a trap. After all, none of this made sense. Not really. Why had Bryant let himself be pursued into a trap? Had he been so certain that Maksutov would be afraid to leave Sitka unprotected?

Darby stood on the icy deck of the Russian ship and gritted his teeth against the chill of snow which fell from the brooding gray blanket of sky.

He was grateful for the Indian furs now and resigned to the probability that he would forever smell like fried fat. At least he was warm and, as the bleak Alaskan sun finally managed to penetrate the land and give it the eerie half-light of the north, he raised a spyglass and began to scan the frigid channel as he had a dozen times in less than an hour.

Suddenly there she was, under full sail and coming straight on in a wild dash for freedom!

Darby spun about and slipped on the deck ice, banging his knee down hard. But he didn't feel a thing as he slid and skittered aft to alert Maksutov and his crew.

He desperately hoped that these Russians could fire their

cannon straight. One thing he knew for certain—Bryant could.

Prince Maksutov ordered his men to the cannons as the ships came sweeping in on one another. Darby returned to the bow calling distances and, when he guessed the ships were less than a thousand yards apart, the *Sea Witch* swung to her starboard side and opened fire.

Through the swirling snow, Darby saw four cannons explode. The writer closed his eyes, certain that, once again, he would be blown into the water. Only this time, the water was cold enough to sustain icebergs and no man could survive its rigors more than a few agonizing minutes.

But Prince Maksutov was a veteran naval officer, one of the few good enough to have survived the Crimean War. So, when the *Sea Witch* swung broadside, he maneuvered his ship so adroitly that Bryant's cannons had only a thin slice of the Russian vessel at which to aim.

The cannonballs missed. Darby heard them pass with a great whooshing sound and then Maksutov ordered his own crew to fire.

Six Russian cannons thundered so loudly that the deck itself jumped and, had he not been gripping the railing, Darby would have been knocked into the freezing ocean. Amid the roar and smoke, he watched two of the cannonballs shatter the port side of the *Sea Witch* and leave gaping holes through her copper-covered hull.

Darby could not believe his eyes. They'd done it! He observed men scrambling about on the already canting decks of the wounded vessel. The ship was listing, out of control but, even so, Bryant fired two more cannons and one nearly scored.

Again, Maksutov shouted an order and Darby glanced back to see sailors madly slamming home wadding and powder. Faces were lit as men huddled to keep them burning in the wind and snow.

A moment passed and then another, as Darby stared so intently that his eyes ached. Finally, as he was about to turn, the Russian cannons roared. Two direct hits at the waterline actually lifted the stricken vessel up in the water. More cannons thundered and her foremast, yards, sail and all, flipped skyward and then crashed to the deck, draping the vessel like a shroud as men cried for mercy across the water.

The tall stump of foremast ripped through the shrouding sail as the wind whipped it furiously across the decks.

"Stop firing!"

Maksutov ordered his cannoneers to trim the sails as the Russian vessel prepared to take on the survivors. It was the only civilized thing to do, even though these were the same men whose laughter had floated across San Francisco Bay while he gripped floating debris and struggled to save lives. Bryant was the real killer among them and, now, the time of justice was almost at hand.

Darby dashed below to his quarters and grabbed a revolver and rifle that Maksutov had loaned him. Then, despite the prince's loud objections, he took his place on the first rescue boat as it pushed away toward the *Sea Witch*. The ocean spray stung Darby's face like pellets of ice as he shuttered his eyes and peered ahead. There was nothing sleek or graceful about Bryant's clipper ship now. She wallowed in the rough seas like a gored and dying animal.

"Hurry!" Darby shouted to the straining oarsmen. They couldn't understand him but he kept yelling it over and over. The ship's stern was beginning to rise. The *Sea Witch* was nearly ready to plunge downward!

The survivors, and there didn't even appear to be as many as a dozen, surged toward the highest point of the decks. Even through the slanting whiteness, Darby could hear them cursing and fighting like rats. A scream blasted across the water as one fell. His body struck the ocean not forty feet from Darby but, before they could reach him, he was gone, the heavy clothing he wore probably pulling him under like a rock.

They were close now. Behind them were three more lifeboats, plenty to rescue everyone if order prevailed and men kept their wits. But as he looked up, he saw a man poised on the outside of the railing, twenty feet up. He was going to jump!

"Wait!" Darby cried. "There's room for everyone!"

Yet, even as he yelled it, the sailor tensed to leap and Darby knew the man would strike the lifeboat with such force that he'd either go through the flooring or capsize them all into the water.

Darby lifted his rifle and pointed it straight up at the terror stricken face of the crewman. He wore a wispy black beard and moustache. His eyes glazed with fear.

"Jump and I'll shoot!"

The man either didn't hear or else the warning snapped whatever thread of reason he'd held onto. He jumped. Darby reversed the weapon and planted his feet. The Russian oarsmen cried out in horror. Darby's timing was split-second and perfect. As the jumper came down, he swung the rifle and knocked him off target just enough to deflect the man's body. His legs slammed across the gunwale and he struck the water.

Darby bent over and pawed at the surface as the head bobbed into view. Then he dragged the unconscious man into the lifeboat. There wasn't even enough time to see if the fool was still alive or not.

The Russians hurled grappling irons up to the men on deck and ropes were strung taut. Like Darby, a Russian in each lifeboat stood up with rifle to shoulder, leaving no doubt that panic would be dealt with in the form of a bullet.

Down they came, wrapping their arms and legs around the thick rope and sliding to safety. When they had all been rescued, Darby waited, then grabbed one of the Americans. "Where's Bryant!" he demanded hoarsely.

"He's gone!"

"Where!"

The sailor spat blood into the ocean. "The bastard had us row him ashore at Skagway! Him with his two sacks bulging with money. Told us the first mate was the captain and we were to run for open sea. That he'd meet up with us next spring."

"Where?"

"Three Saints Bay. Kodiak Island."

"And you believed him!"

"Mister, not one of us *ever* believed him, but that don't mean we were lookin' to die."

Darby looked away, his mouth a tight line of bitter disgust. Of course, this man and the others hadn't tried to stop Bryant. The entire mangy lot of them hadn't the character or leadership to act as a body against such an infamous character.

The lifeboats cast off their ropes and the uninjured Americans didn't need any prodding to exchange places with their captors and row for safety. And, though the lifeboats were heavily laden, the grateful crew of the sinking ship made good work of it in their eagerness to clear the wash of the ocean when it swallowed up the *Sea Witch*.

The clipper obligingly waited until they were a hundred yards distant, then she buried her gaping side-wounds into the ocean, raised her stern with tragic grace and softly slid into a long dive toward the murky depths below.

Every man among them watched in respectful silence. Darby remembered reading an obscure poem of the sea in which it described the death of a ship.

The raging waters grew calm at last
Battle done, victory won,
They clasped the ship forevermore

"Prince Maksutov, I implore you, just a few more hours to Skagway."

"We had a bargain."

"Yes," Darby admitted, "but it was based on the fear that Bryant might race back to Sitka and destroy it before our return. That, we know, could no longer happen."

The prince smiled a half smile. "Tell me," he mused aloud, "if I refuse, what would you do?"

"Ask for the use of your weapons, some food, my harpoon and a lifeboat. Then I'd row to Skagway, if necessary.'' Darby's gaze locked with the Russian's. "If I don't stop the man, he'll be back in the spring. Tougher, more hate-filled.''

"Princess Maria and I will be in Russia.''

"What if some of your people choose to remain in Alaska!" Darby said angrily. "What if the negotiations themselves fail? It has happened before. Do you want that madman to return some night in vengeance?''

Maksutov shook his head. "No," he said. "And that is why I will take you to the village at Skagway and give you anything you need to track him down.''

Darby heaved a deep sigh of relief and then wearily trudged down to his quarters. One more time before he made this final chase north into the Yukon, he was going to climb into a warm bed—stinking furs and all.

The chase, he knew with calm certainty, was almost over.

Chapter 14

Darby waved goodbye to the gawking crowd of Eskimos and turned to bid farewell to Prince and Princess Maksutov.

"Can you handle them?" the princess asked, her fur-encircled face expressing grave doubts.

The writer flourished the long whip in his mittened paw and his ice-crusted moustache bristled with determination as he glared ominously at his awaiting dog team. "They will accept my commands or rue the day!"

"That's the spirit," the prince said. "They must understand who is master."

Darby raised the whip and placed a boot on the runners of the sled. He was ready. "Mush! Mush!" he shouted, cracking the braided sealskin whip over their furry heads.

The dogs bolted from the snow, claws ripping ice. The sled jumped forward, sending the Derby Man crashing to the frozen ground as the dogs shot up the north trail.

"Blast!" he bellowed as the team plunged onward with a throng of Eskimo children in gleeful pursuit. "Blast!"

It was humiliating to hear the natives' laughter and then to have to wait in smoldering silence as the children finally caught the tail-wagging dog team and returned it to Skagway.

But, finally, he was able to get underway toward the pass.

This time, when the dogs left the village, there was no laughter. Only flat skepticism on the part of everyone, convinced that they would never again see the dogs they'd sold nor the great bear of a man in the malodorous furs.

But Darby didn't share their pessimism. He might not be the best musher to race out of Skagway, but he had as

great a determination as anyone who ever started for the
Yukon. And so, late that afternoon when he reached the
pass, he was not unduly surprised to see that Bryant's
sledrunners had left a clear trail, a pair of deep slices in the
soft, clean snow. Darby followed them, staying exactly in
their grooves. His only advantage over the man he pursued
was that he did not have to break trail.

At the base of the pass, he rested and fed the dogs from
a skin-bag of whale fat. There were eight of them, big,
hungry-eyed and tough as rawhide. Maybe the Eskimos
he'd bought them from had merely been driving up the
price, but they'd all sworn that these eight were the
strongest, fastest dogs in Skagway. And Darby was beginning to believe it. They'd pulled his weight almost effortlessly.
He'd long since given up shouting Gee and Haw as they
ignored him anyway and probably couldn't be driven into
breaking their own trail. For his own part, Darby was
content to let them exercise their own little minds as long
as their decisions conformed to his own.

He didn't hate dogs any more than he did horses, but
neither did he feel compelled to hug the howling devils.
Darby peered into the falling snow and took comfort in
noting that the runner-tracks he followed were showing
more and more definition with each mile. When he'd left
Skagway, those tracks had been nearly filled with blown
snow—now they were only half-full.

Darby pitched several more morsels of whale fat into the
dogs' bone-crunching maws and grabbed the sled's handles
as he pointed the beasts up the pass. "Mush! Mush!" he
bellowed, cracking the whip. This time, he held on as the
sled leapt forward and the howling pack of siberian huskies
scrambled up the pass.

Because of his considerable weight, Darby hopped off
the sled almost immediately and hung on at a run. Yet, as
the trail steepened, even the dogs stopped their infernal
howling and settled into a straining pull on their harnesses.
An icy blast of snow and ice slammed into them head-on,
and Darby had a miserable time attempting to keep his
nose from becoming frostbitten.

Up, up they went, climbing from the coast into that first snow-clotted range of passes where only the very tops of the trees showed and the air was like hot needles stabbing tortured lungs.

Over and over, he kept telling the tongue-lolling dogs how fortunate they were not to have to be breaking this trail. The dogs pulled in dejected silence, their heads down and their tails sagging with fatigue.

"The man we follow is heading for Whitehorse," he said aloud. "That's over a hundred miles, but I know you gallant fellows will catch him first. Now mush, you hairy rascals, or we're in for it. Mush!"

The huskies weren't inspired. But at least, Darby thought, they hadn't sat down on him yet. He hoped they felt better than he did.

Every muscle and nerve in his body was screaming when they finally crested the pass. He collapsed, gasping for air, while the dogs sank in their haunches, long pink tongues flecked with foam. It was nearly dark now. They'd all told him not to get trapped on a ridge but to find shelter in a snowbank or perhaps, if he were lucky, a cave.

"Mush. Come on, fellas, get up and mush!"

The dogs rose with snaps and growls. There would be no more lightning starts. The fun was gone from this chase and more than one of the beasts tried to twist about and go back. Darby snapped his whip and got them moving. Ten minutes later, night fell as he plowed blindly down a ridge and crashed into a snowbank.

He could barely move, he was so exhausted. Nevertheless, he forced himself to dig a hole big enough to pack all of them into. They tried to tear the bag of now frozen fat from his hands but he thwarted them and somehow fed them equal shares.

Under the tarpaulin on the sled was his own frozen meat and biscuits. There was even coffee if he could light a fire. But that was impossible. Darby probed about until he found an oilskin wrapper filled with Russian vodka and American cigars. He staggered back into the snow-cave and stepped on a dog's tail. The animal yelped, then sank its fangs into his boot. Darby whacked it across the snout with the back of his gloved hand and the animal retreated with a snarl. Darby ignored the beast and collapsed in the midst of the squirmy pile of dogs and managed to light the cigar. His debilitated senses reeled with pleasure as he uncorked the bottle of vodka and poured a long draught down his throat. He groaned with pleasure.

In the harshness of this frozen nightmare, even the small basic things in life seemed very, very wonderful. He smoked and drank and dreamed of Dolly Beavers while, all about him, the huskies slept and scratched.

It was a long, long night.

Darby awoke to the shrieking wind and, for some time, he lay still in the snow-cave and told himself that it would be better to sleep this day, to gather strength and try to assault the trail when the weather cleared.

But he knew that wasn't possible. Wesley Bryant wasn't far away, not more than five miles. Maybe he'd remain under shelter and wait out the storm, but Darby knew he could not afford that luxury. Bryant's tracks would have been obliterated by the night's snowfall. Perhaps his own team could still follow them, but he'd have to trust their loyalty and intelligence not to route him in a circle back to Skagway.

Darby stirred and one of the huskies growled with menace. The writer grabbed its muzzle and the dog began to squirm helplessly as its friends began thrashing about in wild confusion.

"Listen, all of you!" Darby shouted as he heaved erect and staggered forward out of the cave into the icy wind. "I don't like this any better than you do, but we *are* going on until we catch them."

The dogs peered out of the cave at him and not a tail wagged. Darby stared into their angry brown eyes and felt sweat pop out across his back. They looked like wolves, not sled dogs. Good thing they were all still in harness. Maybe he could control them another day or two, but only if they remained leashed.

"All right," he said in what he hoped was a conciliatory tone, "I know I'm heavier than what you're used to pulling. I can't help it. Just catch the team ahead of us today and I'll not ask for anything more. We'll go home. Understand?"

The throat-rumbling subsided and, one by one, they piled out of the cave, their harnesses remarkably free of tangle.

Quick as he could, Darby fastened them to the sled, not even daring to take his eyes off the team long enough to brush away the heavy layer of fresh snow.

"Mush!" he ordered. When they remained on their haunches, he snapped the whip. Hard. They got up stiffly and the lead dog trotted off on what Darby prayed was the trail to Whitehorse.

The writer plowed through the blizzard until the drifts became so deep and the wind-driven snow so ferocious that his huskies refused to continue. Darby's eyes burned from the glaring whiteness and he no longer could tell whether they were in forest or open country.

That afternoon, it was the dogs who found shelter under the frozen cutback of an Arctic streambed.

Late that second night, he lay staring into darkness, trying to dispel the sense of growing panic which, like the numbing cold, was sucking away at his will. He was lost, he knew that. And the constant blizzards he'd bucked were unusual even by Alaskan standards. He realized he would never make it to Whitehorse, for he'd run out of whale fat and the huskies would not travel hungry. Not for him, at least.

In spite of a fatigue which settled into the very marrow of his bones, Darby knew he was going to lose this chase by default if he didn't overtake Bryant during the next day or two. Perhaps he should have waited until spring and tried to capture or kill Bryant at Three Saints Bay. But deep down, he suspected that was another one of Bryant's ruses; more than likely, the man would never show up.

How far ahead was Bryant at this very moment? Was he

lengthening the distance between them? Darby knew his sole advantage—having a freshly broken trail—was gone now. Bryant was a lighter man and *had* to be a more experienced sledder.

It was time to gamble. And, as he sat crouched among the dogs and puffed on one of his few remaining cigars, Darby decided that he would cache his supplies in this place and mush on with a sled containing only a day's supply of food and his weapons. The harpoon he'd brought seemed one example of something unnecessary, his blankets, eating utensils and extra clothing were others.

Darby reached into his pocket and patted the revolver. He would take this gun and the Russian rifle, although Maksutov had warned him that severe cold and snow might cause them both to malfunction in an emergency. Maybe, Darby thought, I'll take the harpoon, just in case. It saved my life once already.

He waited until he could wait no longer, and then he stood and battled away the snow and moved outside. The first thing he noticed were the stars and the black sky. The second thing was the terrible, aching cold, colder than anything he'd ever believed possible, colder than the inside of a glacier and just as clear.

Moving rapidly in order to stay alive, Darby tore at the ropes covering his sled until he managed to rip away the canvas. By frigid starlight, he threw everything but food, weapons and the harpoon aside and righted the big sled.

"Come on, boys!" he yelled, grabbing a piece of harness and jerking it roughly.

They did not want to leave the snow-cave. He almost had to drag each one out, snapping and biting in protest. Their jaws closed on the heavy furs he wore and Darby felt only numbing pressure as he shoved and crowded them into their places.

"If we don't find them by noon, I promise you it's the end of this, my friends," he told them, wondering if he really could turn back from this chase no matter how much more desperate the odds became with each mile.

He grabbed the whip and made it sing close to their

pointed ears and the snarling dogs fell into a jerky trot as they headed into the freezing winter night.

They began to howl just before daylight and the sound of it made the hair on his bull-neck stand on end. The sound was unlike any he'd ever heard from a dog. Haunting. Chilling. Foreboding and achingly sorrowful.

Darby felt the team pick up speed and his eyes watered and burned as he fumbled under the canvas to grab the rifle. Maybe it was Bryant. If so, the man would be awakened and ready.

It wasn't Bryant, it was one of Bryant's dogs, freshly shot, neatly quartered, then fed to its starving teammates. Darby's huskies sat on their haunches and howled at the cold slice of ice-melon moon. It sent a shiver down the writer's back as he trudged over to inspect what had been Bryant's most recent camp.

There were the remains of a fire under a thatched lean-to of green branches. Darby saw the freshly cut bed of pine boughs and his mouth twisted in bitterness at these small amenities.

The fire was cold but, in this sub-zero temperature, that meant nothing. Besides, as Darby took his hand out of his mitten and plunged it into the ashes, he thought that he could feel *less* cold than the air temperature.

Nearby, the head of the sled dog stared at him with unseeing eyes. It had been shot dead-center through the forehead. Darby recalled how his own team had howled the first night out. Maybe this was the second animal to be sacrificed. Dogs could sense things like that, he'd once been told.

His lead husky, a big white male with shredded ears, whined as if in understanding. Darby trudged back to his sled, his eyes following Bryant's tracks as they disappeared into the black forest, and thinking, He's not far away. I wonder if he knows that I follow.

"Mush," Darby said quietly. The team threw itself into their harnesses; eager to leave this place. And, as if they knew the chase was almost finished, they began to run.

They were still running when a weak sun broke away from the horizon and apologetically hung over the lip of the world. They were still running moments later when the team crested a wind-sculptured ridge and plunged down an icy mountainside with the dogs barking in fear as the sled gathered momentum. Darby tried to slow it, but the ice was hard and fast. He could not get a hold!

Then, he saw Bryant! He was just ahead. Darby cried out in anger and hatred as the man below swung around. His sled was barely under control, but this was instantly forgotten as Bryant leaned forward and snatched up his waiting rifle.

Darby lunged in a desperate attempt to grab his own weapon, but he couldn't reach it and still hang onto the sled which even now was almost overrunning the desperate team. The harness went slack and, as a rifle's bullet cracked over the frozen mountainside, Darby heard the dog team cry out in terror as they used the last of their failing energy to stay just in front of the onrushing sled—a sled which was about to crush them under its merciless steel-edged runners.

Darby had a knife, but to get at it he had to bite his glove and tear his hand free. It seemed to take forever to slash the harness away. The very instant he did, the dogs veered hard as the sled shot by them, hurling down the ice like a runaway locomotive on Wesley Bryant's very own tracks.

The man fired again. Darby crouched on the runners and tried to hang on, as bullets ripped his sled. He fumbled for the revolver in his jacket. His exposed hand was totally numb. The pistol fell between the runners and skated down the mountainside.

My God! he thought in dismal despair, I couldn't have made it easier for him if I'd tried! Helplessly clinging to the runaway sled, and now unarmed, he figured he could count the remainder of his life in a handful of heartbeats.

Bryant's dogs were going crazy and it was all the man could do to hang onto his own rifle. His shots were missing badly. In one smooth motion, Bryant kicked free of his sled, rolled hard and came to a skittering halt with the rifle in firing position.

The writer saw Bryant prop himself up on his elbows and edged slowly backwards, even as the rifle he held began to thunder.

Darby was helpless. He tried to steer the runaway sled toward Bryant but could not budge it from its runner track. He'd miss Bryant by ten feet! Then Bryant would swing around and nail him in the back as he swept by at almost point-blank range.

Darby Buckingham lunged forward and grabbed the only chance he had left in this world—the harpoon. With bullets whining by his sun-blistered cheeks and plucking holes in his stinking fur coat, he drew back the shaft, rooted his feet on the runners and flung the harpoon just as the sled swooped past.

A hundred and fifty yards down the ice, Darby was almost upon the dog sled and Bryant's failing team. With the last of his own great strength, the novelist gripped the sled and then jumped, twisting his body with a terrible violence that made the sled flip into the air, end over end, down the mountainside. Wood splintered and leather bindings were torn like paper ribbons.

Darby felt his own body catapult skyward, then crash to roll. He seemed to roll on and on and came to rest only when he felt a hot breath wash away his own pain. His eyes popped open to stare at the pack of dogs. "You can't eat me!" he yelled. "I'm not dead yet!"

He thrashed into awareness, a cold fear twisting at his insides as the dogs moved into a wary circle about him. Darby coughed and roughly brushed ice from his face, thinking he'd rather die from a bullet than be eaten by. . . .

His lead dog, the great furry white one, hammered its tail on the ice. It whined and lapped him wetly with its immense tongue. The others tried to repeat the act but Darby forced himself to his elbows and stared up the glistening mountainside. He saw Bryant lying on a widening stain of crimson ice. The harpoon jutted from his chest, pinning him like an insect.

144

One of the man's gaunt and hungry dogs began to howl and its companions took up the chorus of death. Darby turned his face away and surveyed his own wagging friends who surrounded him protectively. Dogs *were* dogs. But he'd be blasted if all the hatred he'd seen in their black little eyes wasn't gone now. They almost seemed to be smiling with unspoken gratitude because he'd saved their skins.

The Derby Man glanced once more up at the still form and the harpoon which jutted toward the cold, blue sky. Then he reached out and grabbed that big ugly lead dog and smothered him with gratitude.

"We'll get those other noisy fellas to help. That sled they're tied to is carrying about a million dollars worth of railroad stock we'll be hauling back to civilization. Help me, and we can make it. When we do, I'll buy you and your friends the biggest whalemeat steaks in Alaska."

The howling on the icy mountainside changed to excited barking as the Derby Man stood among the packs of sled dogs. They were telling him everything would be all right.

They *were* going to make it. And somewhere in the blessed heat of Nevada's desert, Charles Crocker and his Union Pacific Railroad were going to make it too.

Author's Note

I grew up in California, but among old-time cowboys like Jonesey, one of the last of a breed of men who could tell me what it felt like to go on a Texas-to-Kansas trail drive. From fellas like that, I learned to ride and rope, to stick a bucking horse or barrel and to admire real cowhands.

That admiration has never dimmed over the years as I've traveled the West in search of stories. The Derby Man has taken me mustanging in Nevada, mining on the Comstock Lode and railroad building over the great Sierra Nevada Mountains. In this novel, I had the fun of learning about San Francisco's Chinatown and tongs, in addition to something about whaling, sailing and sleddog racing.

Through each of the Derby Man episodes, I try to learn more about the men and women who made the West such an exciting frontier. Then I put a twist in the tail of historical fact and let Darby Buckingham play the cards as they happen to fall.

Darby, Dolly Beavers, and now Connor O'Grady are alive for me as their stories unfold. Each is different and, sometimes, it seems as if they take events into their own hands and direct their destinies exactly as they choose. So, in that respect, I guess it's fair to say that I'm sometimes as unsure about how they're going to escape their trials and overcome their enemies as anyone.

I think that's the way it should be. Right now, the Derby Man is recovering back in San Francisco on his long overdue holiday with Miss Beavers. Yet, because it's his good fortune and destiny to chronicle the West, I strongly suspect he is watching the events of his time with great interest. Soon, he'll launch himself at another story which must be told.

When that moment comes, the Derby Man will be equal to the challenge.

⟪⟪ GREAT INDIAN WARRIORS ⟫⟫
WILL HENRY

Will Henry is among the most honored of American historical novelists. His powerful stories of the Great Indian Warriors of the West are alive with the grand spirit and braveries of the Indian people and filled with vivid characters and fascinating details of frontier life.

FROM WHERE THE SUN NOW STANDS
(#14182-1 • $1.95)
They were the greatest fighting Indians of them all, the proud Nez Perce, led by Chief Joseph, a chief of peace in a 1300 mile trek to live as free as they were born. Winner of the prestigious Western Writers of America Spur Award.

THE LAST WARPATH
(On sale February 15, 1982 • #20398-3 • $2.25)
The wild-riding rise and fall of the great Cheyenne people, no tribe lived with fiercer courage or showed more fighting spirit.

CHIRICAHUA (On sale April 15, 1982)
The story of two Apache heroes, one, the war chief loved by his tribe, the other, despised because he scouted for a U.S. Cavalry regiment "to save his people" during the final Apache outbreak to achieve an impossible freedom.

Great stories of the Lone Star frontier

Elmer Kelton's
TALES OF
★
TEXAS

Elmer Kelton is one of the great storytellers of the American West with a special talent for capturing the fiercely independent spirit of his native Texas. Now, for the first time, Bantam Books has collected many of Elmer Kelton's exciting Western novels in a series, TALES OF TEXAS, to be published on a regular basis.

Each of the TALES OF TEXAS is dramatically set in the authentic Texas past. These stories are filled with the special courage and conflicts of the strong men and women who challenged a raw and mighty wilderness and fought to build a frontier legend—Texas.

CAPTAIN'S RANGERS

The Nueces Strip—a stretch of coastal prairie and desert wasteland lying between the two rivers that bordered Texas and Mexico. Long after the Mexican War this parched land remained a war zone, seared by hatred on both sides and torn by lawless raids of looting and burning. By the Spring of 1875 the strip was ready to explode—for this was the year Captain McNelly and his Rangers were sent down from the North. Their mission—"clean up the Nueces Strip."

MASSACRE AT GOLIAD

(Available September 15, 1981)

In 1834 Thomas and Josh Buckalew came to the rugged new country that was Texas. The land that was soon to be ravaged by the battle of the Alamo, at the brutal massacre at Goliad and its bloody sequel, San Jacinto. Because of Thomas' hatred of Mexicans they separated, but the two brothers were re-united when the smoldering violence exploded into savage war.

AFTER THE BUGLES

(Available November 15, 1981)

The Texans had won their war. "Remember the Alamo! Remember Goliad!" Texas no longer belonged to Mexico; it was a free and sovereign republic, rich in land and hope. But it was desperately poor in all other ways. Josh Buckalew knew the problems in Texas had only begun—renegades looking for a gun to steal, Comanches, burned homes, good Mexicans who would likely be shot on sight. Yes, the war was over. But the real battle was still to be won.

(Don't miss Elmer Kelton's TALES OF TEXAS, available wherever Bantam Books are sold.)

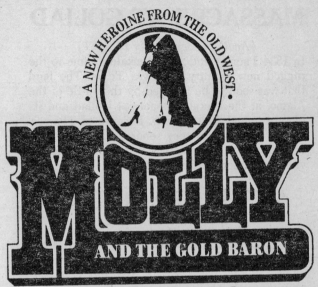

Introducing the first novel in
an exciting new Western series

A NEW HEROINE FROM THE OLD WEST

MOLLY
AND THE GOLD BARON

Stephen Overholser

Meet Molly Owens, an ace operative for the Fenton Investigative Agency sent undercover to crack the most challenging frontier crimes. When she has to be, Molly is as rough as her .38 caliber Colt double-action Lightning model revolver. When she wants to be, Molly's woman enough to melt in a man's arms. In Cripple Creek, Molly is swept up in the West's richest gold strike trying to expose a blackmailer. There's three men after her. One owes her his life, one is trying to kill her and one is falling in love. And just as the case takes a vicious twist towards murder, Molly is plunged in the middle of a deadly mine war that is primed to explode.

#20042-9 • $1.95